IRREVOCABLE TRUST

BY USA TODAY BESTSELLING AUTHOR

MELISSA F. MILLER

BROWN STREET BOOKS

This book is a work of fiction. Names, characters, places, and incidents either are the product of the author's imagination or are used fictitiously.
Any resemblance to actual persons, living or dead, is entirely coincidental.

Published by Brown Street Books.

For more information about the author,
please visit www.melissafmiller.com.

"The Witness Security Program was authorized by the Organized Crime Control Act of 1970 and amended by the Comprehensive Crime Control Act of 1984. The U.S. Marshals have protected, relocated and given new identities to more than 8,500 witnesses and 9,900 of their family members, since the program began in 1971.

...

Witnesses and their families typically get new identities with authentic documentation. Housing, subsistence for basic living expenses and medical care are provided to the witnesses. Job training and employment assistance may also be provided.

...

No Witness Security Program participant, following program guidelines, has been harmed or killed while under the active protection of the U.S. Marshals Service."

—From the U.S. Marshal Service's webpage at http://www.usmarshals.gov/witsec/

1

Allison Bennett was, by nature, a careful woman.

But she'd spent the better part of her adulthood being downright paranoid, and she had vowed to leave that character trait behind when she moved her family to Sunnyvale, North Carolina, for a fresh start.

Old habits had died hard, but after six months in her new home, she'd begun to relax. She stopped sleeping with a loaded gun in her bedside table. She occasionally allowed the gas gauge on her new minivan to dip into the red zone. And once or twice she even forgot to deadbolt the front door.

By the time she'd lived there for nine months, she no longer hyperventilated when her kids disappeared for hours on end, passing long summer days doing whatever it was small-town kids did from dawn until dusk. She depleted her stockpile of canned goods and propane tanks and stopped buying two cases of water every time she shopped for groceries.

She began to feel safe. So safe, in fact, that she allowed herself to believe the past she was running from would never catch up to her.

She decided it was time to put down roots in her new home. So, on her first Christmas as a single mother, she treated herself to a gift.

She called the most trusted supplier of vacuum-packed heirloom seeds in North America and splurged on the largest seed vault it carried: enough to both plant an abundant garden this year and store sufficient seeds to replant in the future just in case society did collapse.

New, non-paranoid Allison chided herself for thinking such a thing, but the extra-large vault was an excellent value for the price, so she went ahead and purchased it anyway.

The seeds arrived, several months later, right on schedule, in plenty of time for planting.

By the time the package landed on her front porch, she'd forgotten all about her plans for a garden. Her new life had turned upside down since Christmas. Just before the new year, the man she was hiding from had escaped from prison, and she'd been paralyzed with fear, waiting for him to show up and ruin the life she'd begun to build. Unable to sleep, she dug the gun out from the storage locker, oiled it, and loaded it. But the days stretched into weeks, which turned into months, and he never appeared.

Finally, she decided not to let the fact that he was out there, *somewhere*, stop her from living. She reminded herself that she was safe. Her kids were safe. He could never find them. She repeated the words the government had told her like a mantra, until, at last, she began to believe them. The gun went back into the storage trunk.

And so when the ground thawed, she spent long hours digging up her lawn, tilling and turning the soil, and amending it to create the perfect environment for her vegetables. She planted her seeds and nurtured them. Her youngest children helped each morning with weeding and watering. The older kids planned elaborate menus around the anticipated harvest. And they all shared her excitement when green shoots peeked out from the rich earth.

None of them knew she'd be dead before the first plant bore vegetables.

2

Monday
Pittsburgh, PA

Sasha McCandless was, by training, a careful woman.

She'd spent the better part of her adulthood in a career where careless mistakes meant the difference between winning a case and losing it. And she'd spent that same amount of time practicing hand-to-hand combat and self-defense.

She'd begun studying Krav Maga because she was a very small person and she wanted to feel capable and strong. She never imagined the training would save her life multiple times, but then she never imagined she'd have so many encounters with murderers. Including the murderer who was currently out there, somewhere, waiting for his chance to strike at her and her new husband.

For the first several weeks after Jeffrey Bricker had hired armed bandits to storm her wedding, she'd been spooked. She kept looking over her shoulder, checking under her car, and generally walking around ready to spring into battle. But Jeffrey Bricker had been out there in the shadows for nearly six months now.

Even her Krav Maga instructor agreed it was unsustainable to live in a state of high alert for an extended period of time. Daniel analogized the situation to the time he'd spent living in Netanya, during a period of heavy conflict between the Israelis and the Palestinians. 'We just accepted that every time we set foot in a public place there was a real risk of a bombing. We scanned the space for suspicious people or packages, made a note of the exits, and went on with our daily lives.'

And, after about a month, so had she and Connelly.

They weren't reckless. It wasn't as if they had forgotten that a megalomaniacal murderer with an actual army at his disposal had escaped from a federal penitentiary with the express goal of killing them. But they couldn't go through life waiting for him to strike, either.

This thought ran through her head as she rapped on the door to her law partner's office. In fact, she tried not to spend time wondering about Bricker's whereabouts except for these weekly briefings. Each Monday, she and her partner, Will Volmer, had a conference call with Hank Richardson, the director of the shadowy nameless federal task force charged with hunting down and capturing Bricker. Connelly sometimes sat in on the calls, too.

She stepped into the office and saw that her husband had beaten her there.

Will and Connelly had their heads bent over the phone. They both looked up as she closed the door behind her. She raised her coffee mug in greeting.

"Sasha's here," Will announced into the speaker phone while Connelly slid off the edge of Will's desk and came over to greet her with a chaste kiss.

His arm lingered around her waist. Six months

of marriage hadn't dulled the thrill that ran down her spine at the contact.

"Morning, Hank," she craned her neck toward the speaker.

"Sasha," his familiar voice boomed through the phone.

She inched one of Will's guest chairs closer to the desk and took a seat. Connelly followed suit.

"What do you have for us, Hank?" Connelly asked.

"Nothing new, I'm afraid. I've increased the team, adding people from across six agencies. We're still out there chasing down leads, but, so far, he's a ghost."

"What about the prepper group in New Mexico?" she asked.

Two weeks earlier, a low-level marijuana dealer had been picked up in a Drug Enforcement Agency sweep. He'd been eager to get a deal and had started rattling off the names of his suppliers and his buyers. He mentioned that he had some regular customers who were foot soldiers in a local militia group. Further questioning by the DEA agents led to the revelation that the group was rumored to be harboring a fugitive who'd escaped from prison.

At the previous week's briefing, Hank had said

the DEA and Homeland Security were planning a joint raid on the compound. It was the most promising lead they'd had in months.

"After much consultation, the agencies agreed that the DEA did not have cause to raid the group. They then reached out to Alcohol Tobacco & Firearms. While the ATF has been interested in seizing the groups cache of weapons for some time, after due consideration, they determined that the risk of a Ruby Ridge or Waco scenario was too high. So, the desk jockeys in charge are all punting. While everyone was bickering over who was going to do what, if anything, I went ahead and authorized a mission by a ... freelancer ... who could only confirm that, if Bricker had been there, he's gone now."

Hank's tone left no question as to his views about the bureaucratic maneuvering that may have allowed Bricker to slip through the government's fingers. It also made clear that she shouldn't ask for further details about the 'freelance mission.'

Given that she was married to one of Hank's freelancers, she knew all too well that the mission was likely technically illegal.

"Next time," she said.

Connelly rubbed her arm reassuringly through her thin, cotton cardigan. "That's the attitude."

"Well, I'll sign off now," Hank said.

"Anything else? What about the prison dentist who helped Bricker escape?" Will asked.

Originally classified as a hostage, the dentist, who had ties to Bricker's militia, was now officially considered an accomplice. He was either dead—likely at Bricker's hands—or on the run.

"There's no news on Dr. Rumson."

She caught Connelly's eye and flashed him an encouraging smile as Hank said his goodbyes.

Will depressed the conference button to end the call and searched her face.

"Are you sure you're okay?" he asked.

"I'm fine."

They'd done everything in their power to secure the office—new alarm system, new locks, and new Connelly-enforced rule that Sasha wasn't to work late into the night alone. She knew Will was almost as worried as she and Connelly were, but there was no way to guarantee Bricker wouldn't storm the office.

Or her condo. Or her parents' place. Or her hairdresser's salon.

Of course, it was unsettling, not knowing where Bricker was or what he was planning. Every week, the news was the same: Bricker was still out there somewhere, hiding, watching and waiting for a chance to strike. But eventually he'd make a mistake.

3

Sunnyvale, North Carolina

Officer Vince Fornier scratched his left ear and watched Lilah Stokes' face.

He was trying to reserve judgment about the pointless nature of this particular call, but everyone in town knew Lilah was an unrepentant gossip with an overactive imagination—and nosy, to boot.

Everybody also knew that it had nearly driven her mad when the Bennett woman and her six kids showed up in town a year and half ago and moved in right next door to her. Allison Bennett was as close-lipped as Lilah was gabby. She kept to herself and never bothered to address any of the rumors swirling around town about her.

Was she divorced? Widowed? A single mother? Did she work? Was she on welfare? Or was she independently wealthy? Nobody knew.

Nobody knew anything about Allison or her kids. They hadn't joined a church, a social club, a sports team, or a volunteer organization since landing in Sunnyvale. She didn't even send her children to school. According to the registrar, she'd filed papers saying she was homeschooling them instead.

Most people would have realized the Bennetts were reserved and left it at that. But not Lilah. Allison's reticence had only served to fuel Lilah's curiosity—some might even call it an obsession.

In fact just a month earlier, the Bennett woman had called in to report a suspected prowler after her trash cans had been knocked over in the middle of the night. Vince had answered that call, too.

After canvassing her property, he'd assured Allison that there was no one hiding in her yard. Despite being sorely tempted, he didn't mention that he'd seen Lilah racing into her garage, clutching her robe around her, when he'd pulled up.

Now, he just listened as the old busybody explained why she was worried about her next-door neighbor.

"Are you listening to me, Vincent? I was weeding my begonias when something caught my eye. I looked through the Bennetts' living room window and saw a woman's foot and leg sticking out from behind the sofa. I rapped on the glass but the woman didn't move. So, I walked around to the front and rang the bell. No one answered the door."

Vince let his eyes drift to the flower bed in question and then return to her face. Surely she knew he could tell just by looking at the layout that she couldn't have seen into the Bennett house from her flower bed.

She'd been spying on her neighbor. Again.

She glared back at him.

Finally he said, "I'm sure she's just resting or something. But I'll check it out. Why don't you go on in and get ready for your card club meeting."

"You never were the brightest of the bunch, Vincent. Who on earth lays down to *rest* on the living room floor? She probably passed out drunk. Or she overdosed on drugs. Or maybe she fell and hit her head—"

He ignored the insult and raised a calming

hand to stem the tide of horrible fantasies she was spewing.

"Now, Mrs. Stokes, I said I'm going over there to check it out. You've satisfied your civic duty. Go back inside."

She shot him a look that could've curdled milk then slammed the door shut in his face.

He tipped his hat at the closed door and chuckled to himself as he started down the steps to the sidewalk.

He leaned on Allison's doorbell just in case she had fallen asleep, but she didn't answer. He tromped through her freshly mulched bushes and pressed his face up against the glass in the large window. Just as Lilah had described, he saw a shapely pale leg and a bare foot protruding from behind the floral-patterned couch.

Then he spotted the glossy red slick of blood seeping into the carpet beside the woman's leg. A lot of blood.

His heart leapt into his throat, and he fumbled for his radio until he remembered the Chief was out of town, taking his annual week's vacation up at the lake. He was going to have to handle this on his own.

He tried to force the window up, but it was locked tight and, judging by the layers of paint over the frame, probably painted shut, too. He vaulted, one-handed, over the fence enclosing the backyard, and tried the kitchen door. The screen door swung open right away and the interior door was unlocked.

He forced himself to slow his breathing as he drew his gun and searched his memory for the proper technique to sweep a house for intruders. It wasn't a maneuver he'd had much occasion to use since graduating from the police academy.

He burst into the kitchen and aimed his gun in a smooth arc around the room. Empty.

"Ms. Bennett? It's Officer Fornier. Are you okay, ma'am?" he called into the living room. He was pleased and surprised to hear that his voice didn't crack.

She didn't respond. He headed toward the living room.

He hurried over to the body behind the couch and scanned the large room to confirm no one else was there.

As he neared the body, he pulled out his radio to call for the town's ambulance. One look at what was left of Allison Bennett's face was all he needed to know that an ambulance would be futile. He radioed the station and told dispatch to call in the coroner instead.

Then he crouched on shaky legs beside the corpse. Her long, straight hair fanned out behind her. Someone had beaten her so ferociously that what was left of her face had caved in on itself. Her cheekbones flattened and smashed. Dark blood caked her hairline. To confirm what he already knew, he placed two fingers on the inside of her limp wrist. She had no pulse.

Bile rose in his throat and he stood quickly, gulping for air. The cloying scent of blood heated by the afternoon sun filled his nose. Sweat beaded his brow as he struggled to regain his composure.

He had to get out of there.

Secure the scene.

He raced out of the room and began to move methodically from one room to the next, searching every closet, corner, and behind every curtain. He checked the basement and even lowered the pull-down access to check the attic crawl space.

Once he'd satisfied himself that he was alone in the home except for a dead woman, he reluctantly forced himself to go back toward the living room. His heavy footsteps echoed through the still house as he walked slowly down the hallway.

He hovered just outside the doorway into the room. Procedure required him to wait for the coroner, but he sure as heck didn't want to have to look at Allison while he waited. He already knew her ruined face was going to haunt his dreams.

The sound of childish laughter in the backyard caught his ear. He hurried to the kitchen door and peered through the glass.

The Bennett children were tromping through the yard. The tallest two were in the front, carrying a cooler between them. Behind them, the middle two wrestled with three fishing rods apiece. And the little two brought up the rear, shouting and hooting.

He raced outside and skidded to a stop just outside the door.

The two oldest kids froze mid-step at the sight of a police officer running out of their home. They let the cooler fall to the ground with a thud.

The other four children eyed him with varying degrees of curiosity and fear.

He cleared his throat and tried to think of something reassuring to say.

Lilah, bless the old bat, saved him.

She opened her door and called over the fence, "I just made a batch of brownies. I don't suppose anyone over there wants to help me eat them?"

The little ones squealed and headed for the gate.

"Wait," the girl with the fishing rods yelled after them. "We have to check with Mom first!"

Vince found his voice.

"It's okay. You kids go on over to Mrs. Stokes' place. Go on, now. Get."

The middle two, hesitated, but placed the rods on the ground."

"Go ahead," the oldest girl told them. "We'll be over in a minute."

After they walked away and closed the gate behind them, the remaining two children stared at Vince expectantly.

He tried to keep his expression neutral, devoid of any hint of the horror that waited inside the house.

"What's going on?" the boy demanded.

Vince shuffled his feet and tried to decide whether they were old enough that he could just tell them a sanitized version of the truth. But he was a terrible judge of kids' ages. They could have been anywhere between twelve and eighteen. He eyed them again. He was pretty sure the boy was the older of the two.

"How old are you and your sister, son?"

"I'm sixteen and a half, officer. She's almost fifteen."

The kid answered right away, in a serious voice,

like he knew what Vince was thinking and wanted to convince him they were adult enough to handle whatever he had to say.

Vince wasn't so sure about that. His stomach was still turning from the sight of their beaten mother.

The girl squinted at him hard and twirled a strand of hair around her finger, wrapping it tighter and tighter as she stared at him.

"So, uh, you guys catch anything?" He gestured toward the fishing poles and cooler.

"No. A couple small mouths and a sunny. Too small. We threw them back," the boy answered in a clipped, but polite, tone.

He threw his sister a meaningful look. "Hey, Brianna, why don't you put the fishing gear up in the shed?"

She glared back at him for a long moment.

Vince couldn't read the look that passed between them, but it was clear they were having an entire, possibly heated, conversation without saying a word.

"Fine." She forced the word out from between clenched teeth and stomped off toward the abandoned rods.

The boy waited until she hoisted the poles over her shoulder and disappeared into the small white shed. Then he fixed Vince with a grim look.

He dug through a duct-tape wallet with shaking fingers and pulled out a dog-eared business card.

"Here. Call this Hank Richardson guy," the kid said in a matter-of-fact voice.

"Why?" Vince asked, turning the card over in his fingers and puzzling over the lack of a title or business name on the card. It simply read *Hank Richardson* and listed a telephone number.

The kid choked out the words. "He said to call him if anything ever happened to my mom. She's dead, isn't she?"

4

Leo was cooling his heels at Sasha's office, waiting to see if she could join him for lunch when Hank's text hit his phone:

Need to see you. Just you. Urgent. @ Babs' in 10.

Luckily, Babs' Place, the newest, hip cocktail bar to join the urban revitalization effort, was a short walk from the office, just across the pedestrian bridge to East Liberty.

Hank was already there, camped out in a booth near the back. It was the ideal spot, with a clear line of sight to the front and far enough away from the bar's only other midday occupants—a couple nuzzling one another in the corner, and a guy who looked like a refugee from the set of Mad Men relishing a martini at the end of the bar.

Leo slid into the booth beside Hank. He didn't

care how it looked, he had no intention of sitting with his back to the door either.

"I took the liberty of ordering for you." Hank nodded to the short glass of scotch on the table, then lifted his own whisky glass in a salute.

It really wasn't Leo's style to have drinks in the middle of a weekday, but Hank knew as much, so if he figured an exception was in order, an exception was probably in order.

Leo let the amber liquid coat his throat with a satisfying burn before he spoke.

"Johnny Walker Blue? Are we celebrating something?"

Hank examined his glass. "We're paying our respects. Seems like that calls for the good stuff."

"Who died?"

"Enjoy your drink. I'll tell you in a minute."

Leo frowned. "Why the cloak and dagger routine?"

Hank barked out a humorless laugh. "We're federal agents, son. If we don't do the cloak and dagger stuff, who will?"

"You're a federal agent," he reminded his boss. "I'm a ..."

What was he? A former air marshal. A former security chief. A current operator for a nameless section of the federal government, so secret that it operated without protection of law.

"Consultant," Hank supplied.

"Fine. I'm a government consultant. So tell me who's dead. Is it Bricker?"

"No such luck. It's Allison Bennett." Hank sighed heavily.

Allison Bennett? Leo searched his memory, but came up blank.

"Do I know her?"

"Allison Bennett, formerly known as Anna Bricker, was brutally murdered in her North Carolina home."

Leo's blood turned to ice in his veins as a chill shot through him.

"*Anna Bricker?* He found her? Are the kids okay? How did he find her?"

"Whoa, whoa, whoa. Slow down. We don't know that Bricker killed her." Hank held up his hand like a crossing guard.

"Come on."

"I'm serious. Don't jump to conclusions."

Leo decided to let that go for now, even though he didn't think it was a huge leap of logic to assume as a starting point that the murdered estranged wife of a vengeful murderer had been killed by her husband. Thinking about husbands and wives led to another line of questioning.

Why are you cutting Sasha and Will out of the loop?"

"They don't have the security clearance needed to be privy to this conversation."

"It affects them, too, Hank."

"I'm serious, Leo. You do not have permission to share any of the details of this conversation with Sasha."

Leo sipped his drink and bit back his response. Hank didn't stand on ceremony. If he didn't want Sasha and Will to know something, there was probably a good reason. That didn't mean he had to like it, though.

Hank pressed on. "You need to understand the gravity of this situation."

"I think we all understand the situation, Hank. Jeffrey Bricker's wife's been murdered, and we have no idea how he got to her or where he is. Assuming he did it, of course," he added as an afterthought for the sake of appearance.

"It's much bigger than that," Hank said.

Leo waited.

"You realize that WITSEC takes security extremely seriously, right?"

"Sure."

That was an understatement. Even though he had been a highly-placed federal marshal before his retirement, he'd never set foot in the building devoted to WITSEC until he and Hank had accompanied Anna Bricker and her children there for their intake evaluations.

WITSEC—known to the general public as the federal Witness Protection Program—was, by design, a black box. He doubted there were a hundred people in the entire government who knew the precise location of the orientation center. He wasn't one of them.

He, Hank, Anna, and her six children had been whisked to the center in van with blackout windows. The driver parked in an underground garage and ushered the nine of them into a windowless building. The set up reminded him either of going to a conference at the world's bleakest resort hotel or being confined in a very posh prison. It was a toss-up.

During their time there, the Brickers never encountered another witness in a hallway or conference room. They slept in a two-room suite and spent their days meeting with counselors, agents, psychologists, and prosecutors—all of whom were charged with transitioning the family members to their new identities and helping them establish their new lives. Every aspect of the program was devoted to preserving the witnesses' anonymity. Only the WITSEC inspector assigned to relocate them would know where they would be placed.

In fact, Leo was never told the Brickers' new names or where they'd been relocated. As far as he knew, Hank hadn't been told either.

"Are you even sure it's Anna?"

Hank nodded glumly. "It's not yet confirmed. I'm flying down there this afternoon."

"Down where? Why don't you start at the beginning?"

"Here's what I know. Anna and her six children were relocated in January 2013. A woman named Allison Bennett was found beaten to death in Sunnyvale, North Carolina, earlier today. The police officer who discovered her body called me directly because the dead woman's oldest son handed him my business card and told him to call me."

"And you think Bennett is Anna Bricker?"

"I do. Same initials—which is standard operating procedure for WITSEC. They want to make it easy for the witnesses to remember their new names. Also, this woman moved to Sunnyvale in

January 2013, according to the officer. And she has six kids. No husband."

Leo pulled a face. "That's still pretty thin, Hank."

"Maybe. But this kid got my card somewhere, and I don't make a habit of handing it out. But I did give it to Anna's oldest boy, Clay, before we left them at the center."

"You did?"

"I told him that he was the man of the family now. I said his mom would have a number to call at WITSEC if she ever felt that they were in danger, but he should feel free to call me if anything ever happened to her."

Leo's heart sank. "The kid's the right age?"

"Officer Fornier said he's sixteen and a half. That's the right age. And his name's Cole. Same initial."

"Coincidences happen," he said even though he didn't believe it.

"They do," Hank agreed. He drained his glass. "But we both know this is no coincidence. And Fornier said the beating was brutal, like it was personal."

There was no doubt Bricker was capable of it. This was a man who'd shot a sheriff's deputy in the face. A man who hired armed bandits to storm a wedding. A man who'd carried the deadliest virus on the planet around in a vial in his duffel bag. A little bludgeoning, face-bashing, and mayhem were right up his alley.

"So what now?"

"I'm going to go down there and sit on those kids."

"What?"

Hank spoke slowly. "In more than forty years, no one has ever successfully tracked down a witness in WITSEC. It simply doesn't happen. They pride themselves on that—a witness who enters the program and follows the rules is perfectly safe. For life. Well, that perfect record's just been shattered into a million pieces, and it's enough to make a cynic wonder if Bricker had inside help."

"You're not serious."

Hank spread his big palms wide. "Is it really so crazy?"

Leo didn't know how to answer that. On the one hand, *yes*, it was insane to think that a WITSEC inspector would dime out the very people he was sworn to protect. On the other hand, how else could Bricker have gotten to his wife?

He dodged the question. "What does WITSEC say?"

"I haven't spoken to anyone at WITSEC yet. As far as I know, they don't even know she's dead yet."

"What?" Leo yelped.

Hank glared at him, and he lowered his voice. "Sorry. What?"

"Well, standard operating procedure would be for the inspector who placed them to get a call from either the family or local law enforcement—if they even know who she was. Some of these marshals can be pretty sloppy about the details—it's not unheard of for them to fail to notify the locals when they relocate a witness, especially one like Anna Bricker, who wasn't a criminal herself. The kid didn't call WITSEC, and I highly doubt Fornier did."

"Based on what?"

"Based on the fact that he spoke to me. WITSEC would have told him not to."

Leo nodded. He had a point there. WITSEC, with its great love for secrecy, never would have let some local cop call up Hank and discuss the murder of a witness."

"Okay, well, why haven't you called them? Isn't it also SOP to move the kids once a threat's been identified?"

Leo was stunned that Hank was playing so

loose with the rules. Sure, that's what they did, but these were *kids.*

"I don't know whether that procedure would apply. Those kids weren't witnesses. They were only in the program because their mom testified. She's gone. Six minors? What's their legal status? Who's supposed to take over as guardian? Some WITSEC inspector back in D.C.? It's going to be a mess. It'll take ages to get it all ironed out. And in the meantime, Bricker's out there, and there's a chance he got to Allison through either the negligence or the malfeasance of a marshal assigned to WITSEC."

"So, what? You're an army of one?"

"Yes."

"I'm coming with you,"

"No, you're not. Don't worry, I'm not going to let anything happen to those kids."

Leo gave Hank a long look.

"You know if Bricker wanted those kids dead, they'd already be dead, right? He's probably trying to lure us into a trap."

"I know. That's why you're staying put. For now, you need to keep Sasha and Will as far away from this as you can."

"Sure, give me the hard job."

Hank cracked a weak smile and signaled the bartender for another round.

"MAC, truthfully, I have no idea what Leo's up to." Naya looked up from her Contracts outline and eyed Sasha with visible exasperation.

Usually, Naya prided herself on being the heartbeat of McCandless & Volmer, Attorneys at Law—a status that extended to its attorneys' business *and* personal lives. She knew the names of all their clients, could rattle off who was behind on invoices and who just moved to new office space. She had friends all over town, at other firms, within the court system, at private investigators' offices. She also knew their birthdays, their secret fears, and what they wanted for their birthdays. Under ordinary circumstances, yes, if Connelly was keeping secrets from Sasha, Naya would have known about it.

But these were not ordinary circumstances. It was May. Final exam time at Duquesne University School of Law. And Naya was not only the firm's legal assistant, administrator, and jack of all trades. She was a first-year law student. And, by definition, currently a crazy person.

Sasha and Will had taken to calling her the 'lawbie' behind her back, because she'd become a dead-eyed legal-element-spouting zombie.

They could both remember their first year exams, so they weren't overly worried about her hair-trigger temper, lack of attention to personal appearance, or the mumbling of doctrines of law under her breath. It was a temporary condition. They treated her like a caged lion, only instead of feeding her raw steaks, they tossed takeout containers and mugs of coffee into her office and then retreated.

In fact, as she recalled her own first year exams, a wave of guilt crashed over Sasha.

"You're right. I'm sorry to bother you during exams."

Naya waved her hand in a *don't worry about it* gesture. As she did so, the pink highlighter she was holding hit her cheek and left a thick line down the side of her face.

"You have—" Sasha stopped herself mid-sentence. There was no point in mentioning it. Naya's Contracts final was in three hours. She was unlikely to stop studying long enough to go to the bathroom let alone to scrub the bright pink mark off her face.

Naya stared up at her, waiting.

"Anyway, good luck. Let me know if you need a refill." Sasha pointed toward the coffee teetering precariously on a stack of hornbooks.

"Thanks."

Naya turned back to her review of offer and acceptance and shut out all distractions, namely Sasha.

Sasha tiptoed out of the office and pulled the door shut silently.

She'd just have to use her powers of persuasion to convince Connelly to open up to her. That approach didn't sound all bad. She grinned to herself.

5

Cole Bennett narrowed his eyes at Mrs. Stokes, who was hovering uncertainly, half on the front porch, half in the doorway. She was nervous. He could tell by the way she kept twirling her wiry gray hair around her finger. All of his sisters did that same thing when they were anxious. Funny thing was, his mom had never done that.

Mom.

His heart squeezed in his chest.

"We're not leaving." He planted his feet in a wide stance and puffed out his chest.

She tried to peer around him to get a glimpse of Calla and Hal, the youngest of his siblings and the only two who didn't have the sense to make themselves scarce when the doorbell rang. Instead they were peeking out from the hallway and giggling.

"Honey, I understand you're all probably in shock right now. It's a terrible thing, what happened to your mother, but you're only seventeen, right?" She crossed herself at the mention of his mom.

Technically, he wouldn't be seventeen for another five months, but he figured older was better in this situation.

"That's right."

"How are you going to take care of all your brothers and sisters all by yourself?"

"We'll manage."

She smiled hesitantly. "But you don't have to do it by yourself. There are programs—"

He held up a hand to stop her. Despite himself, he flashed back to his father and recalled the way he squared his shoulders and jutted his chin when he was asserting his authority. Cole adopted the mannerisms that had worked so well for his dad.

"Listen. We don't want your help. We're fine."

"You need an adult to take care of you, son."

"Our ... uh, Uncle Hank is on his way," Cole said. He figured a partial truth was good enough for Mrs. Stokes.

"Uncle? What about your father? Is he in the picture?"

"That's none of your business, you old snoop."

She opened and closed her mouth, like a fish flailing on the bank after it had been landed.

He closed the door before she could find her voice. Then he engaged the deadbolt and turned to lean against the door. He reached inside his waistband to confirm his mom's old gun was still there. He'd dug it out of the trunk while the others were still wandering around the house in shock. He hoped he wouldn't have to use it, but if that old bat showed up with a social worker, he'd do whatever it took to keep his family together.

You're just like him. The thought buzzed across his mind like a gnat. He swatted it away. He was nothing like his dad. If anything, he was the opposite: if he resorted to violence, it would be to keep his family together, not to tear it apart.

He steadied his breathing and looked up. Calla and Hal were sitting cross-legged in the doorway to the kitchen, staring at him. Brianna, Leah, and Mark emerged from the upstairs hallway and peered down over the railing at him.

For a moment, all six of them were quiet.

His eyes met Brianna's.

She looked back at him for a second before she nodded.

"Family meeting," she said.

They all filed into the dining room and took a seat around the long oak table. It was where they ate, prayed, learned, and played. And where their mother had always convened family meetings.

Cole's throat felt tight when he looked at her empty chair, but he pushed thoughts of her out of his mind. Right now, he had to figure out a way to keep them together. That was his job. He could cry later, in the shower—the only truly private space in a house of six people. Now, he had to lead.

Brianna tapped his arm.

He turned to face her. Her green eyes were clouded with worry and sadness. She looked way older than fourteen suddenly.

"They don't remember," she whispered.

"Neither of them?"

"Neither," she confirmed.

They hadn't been sure whether Calla and Hal had any memories of their previous life—their old names, the compound, their dad. They knew Leah and Mark remembered, but none of them ever talked about it. Now, with their mom gone, he wasn't sure how much to tell the others. Brianna said she'd find out what the little ones knew. Apparently nothing.

That was good and bad. Good because it was safer that way, but bad because they wouldn't be able to understand how much danger they were really in.

They were at war with their dad. And the government hadn't yet shown up to protect them.

Cole wet his lips and tried to think of the best way to explain the situation.

Brianna beat him to it.

"Okay, guys," she said in a no-nonsense voice that sounded just like their mom's. "Here's the deal. We only have each other now. It's just us. And because we don't have a mom or dad, some people are going to want to take over, try to help us."

"Help is good," Leah said with the wisdom of someone who hasn't yet celebrated her tenth birthday.

"Help *can be* good," Brianna agreed. "But we don't want this help."

"Why not?" Leah asked.

Mark exploded. "Because we'll end up in foster care or an orphanage or something—they'll try to split us up!"

"An orphanage? Like in 'Annie'?" Calla asked.

"Will Daddy Warbucks be our new dad?" Hal said, bouncing in his seat.

"Can we get a dog?" Calla added.

Cole threw Brianna a look. They'd already lost control of the discussion. *Now what?*

"No dog, no orphanage, and especially no new dad," she told them firmly.

Calla stuck out her lower lip.

Brianna ignored the pouting and continued, "We have to be a team. And we have to be very careful. Nobody goes outside without me or Cole."

"Not even to the backyard?" Leah asked.

"Is the backyard outside?" Cole said.

"Yeah."

"Then no," he said, trying to keep his voice even like Brianna's. There was no point in terrifying them, but they had to understand that this was serious.

"What about food?" Mark wanted to know.

"What about it?" he countered.

"When we run out of food, who's going to go to the store? And who's going to cook? And where are we going to get money to pay for it?" Mark's voice began to tremble as the adult concerns that now faced them started to become real.

Brianna held up both hands. "Take a deep breath," she soothed. She waited until he did as she said, then she continued, "Cole and I are going to take care of everything, we promise. We just need you to help. You have to listen to us and do what we say, okay?"

She swept her gaze around the table. Four heads nodded in unison.

"Good," she said.

Mark, at twelve, wasn't as easily satisfied as the three youngest. "But what's the long-term plan? We have a plan, right?"

Cole nodded. "Of course, we have a plan. Hank is going to help us."

"Who's Hank? Is he our uncle?" Leah wanted to know.

Cole couldn't tell her no, not after she'd just heard him tell the busybody next door that he was. "Yep, Uncle Hank is on his way."

Brianna gave Mark an encouraging smile. "See? It's going to be fine." She turned to the others. "Now, who wants pizza for dinner?"

6

Jeffrey Bricker's legs were cramping. And he had to urinate.

But he couldn't risk getting up to stretch, let alone relieve himself—not until nightfall, when the other campers were sleeping. The state park he'd chosen was a good fifty miles outside Sunnyvale, but he had to assume that Anna's body had been found by now and that someone had discovered her real identity. If so, then there would be all-point-bulletins out through the Southeast to be on the lookout for him.

He distracted himself from his discomfort by recounting how flawlessly he'd executed his plan —and his wife.

It had been simple, really.

He knew Anna better than any other human alive. He knew that eventually she'd give in to her longing for a garden. He also knew that the survival tactics he'd introduced her to weren't ingrained, not really. If they had been, she never would have left the compound and turned on him. So he surmised that, in her weakness, Anna wouldn't recognize the danger in doing business with someone he knew; he thought she would contact one of the movement's trusted suppliers of heirloom seeds—and there were only three major companies who supplied most of the patriot groups. He'd been right on both counts.

He'd planned to call the owners of all three companies. But he'd only had to call the first company on his list. Gary Stevens had fallen all over himself to help. Why wouldn't he? Jeffrey was the hero of the American prepper movement. True patriots through the Western Hemisphere were lining up to help him any way they could.

Stevens was glad to provide Jeffrey with a list of customers who fit his specifications: new customers; female; ordering the largest vault (Anna never could pass up a deal).

It had then been an easy matter to take the list to the public library in Arizona and start typing the names into the Google search bar. He ran the entire list of names and addresses through Google, even though he knew he'd hit pay dirt with the third name on the alphabetized list.

Allison Bennett had no Internet footprint. None. She wasn't on Facebook. She had never commented on a blog post. She'd never been photographed. And according to publicly available records in the Pape County Recorder of Deeds Office, Ms. Bennett had purchased her home in January of 2013.

Jeffrey was disappointed in how easy she'd made it.

After crisscrossing the country through a system of stops on the movement's version of the Underground Railroad, he reached Sunnyvale and scouted out the town.

He'd spent two nights sleeping in the shed behind the 'Bennett' family's house, watching their movements through the small plastic window by day to get a sense of their routines. At dusk, he crept up to the dusty loft at the top of the shed, ate two energy bars, and then bunked down under an old tarp that had been left there.

He'd expected to feel some melancholy or longing as he watched his children trot through the backyard, tending the garden and playing tag, but he hadn't.

He'd noted with approval that Clay had grown several inches and had become broad-shouldered. Bethany seemed taller, too, and she'd gotten braces. Henry and Clara had lost their baby fat. Lacey looked exactly as he remembered her. So did Michael, but when Jeffrey heard him call across the yard to his sister, he was surprised that his middle son's voice cracked. Puberty, already?

He noted the changes in his children clinically, but he felt ... nothing. Nothing at all.

Until, that is, he saw Anna.

She was hanging laundry out to dry. The spring wind whipped her hair into her eyes and wrapped her long skirt around her ankles.

She looked older than he remembered—more gray in her hair, more lines on her face—and sadder. But his throat tightened at the sight of her, and, despite her spineless betrayal, he had to fight an urge to go to her and gather her up in his arms.

But Bricker was a disciplined man, and a patient man, so he stayed in his hiding spot and waited for the time to be right.

Very early on the morning of his third day hunkering down in the shed loft, Lacey and Henry came banging into the shed to grab fishing poles and tackle boxes. He watched from under the tarp as they hauled out the equipment. Then he waited until all six kids had lugged the equipment through the yard and disappeared down the hill below, Clay in the lead and Bethany bringing up the rear, with Clara up on her shoulders.

After he could no longer hear their shouts and laughter, he did some jumping jacks and push-ups to get his heart pumping. Then he scanned the shed for potential weapons.

Axe. Hedge clippers. Shovel.

He considered and dismissed each in turn. He found what he was looking for on Anna's potting bench. A small, heavy trowel with a graphite handle. He recognized it as the one she'd used back at their old home. He'd shoved it in his back pocket and pushed open the door.

He breathed in deeply, filling his lungs with the crisp, morning air. Then he crept through the backyard toward the kitchen door. As he expected, it was unlocked. He slipped inside, shaking his head at Anna's basic security failures.

He heard the shower running upstairs, so he poured himself a cup of coffee and sat down at the table to wait for his wife.

He grinned to himself now, remembering the fear and surprise in her eyes when she'd seen him sitting there. He replayed the scene, relishing each moment. Her screams, her mad dash for the living room, the satisfying thumping sound her face made as it collapsed.

He wished he'd been able to spend more time with her, afterward. But he'd known he'd had to hurry. Even at their most disorganized, the federal authorities would be swooping in to scoop up his children by nightfall. Ultimately, he planned to free them from their governmental shackles, too. He'd be damned if a corrupt, collapsing government was going to hold his kids hostage indefinitely. But he had a plan to execute in order of priority, and it was time to make his next move.

He slipped out the back door and melted into the woods behind the house.

He hiked at a good clip and set up his temporary camp hastily. He didn't intend to waste much more time in the backwoods of North Carolina. He'd eat and rest. Before the first morning light, he'd break camp and head for the next stop on the Patriot Railroad. Destination: Pittsburgh, Pennsylvania.

7

Sasha smiled and nodded at Bertie. Her hand-to-hand combat instructor's mother was recounting the plot of a movie she'd recently seen, but between the buzz of conversation, the music at full volume, and the traffic rushing by below the balcony, Sasha could hear every third word—if that.

Daniel and Chris had been hosting their weekly wine tastings for two months, now, and they'd grown from an intimate gathering of close friends to a mad crush of people. Last week's feature in the *City Paper* had only increased their popularity.

Bertie leaned closer and shouted, "You seem distracted. Is everything okay?"

Sasha sipped the assertive Spanish red that was

the star of this week's party and considered her response. Everything was decidedly *not* okay.

Connelly was keeping secrets.

After vanishing on her for lunch, he'd turned up at the condo reeking of booze just before the party. Then he barely spoke to her on the short walk to Daniel and Chris's place, lost in his own thoughts.

She searched through the crowd and spotted him in a tight group gathered in the space between the French doors and the piano in the living room. He didn't seem to be paying any attention to the conversation around him. He was staring at the wall over the fireplace, his jaw clenched tightly.

Her chest ached at the sight of him looking so fiercely unhappy. She almost sighed then caught herself. Bertie was waiting for an answer.

"I'm sorry, Bertie. I'm just a little tired, that's all."

Bertie narrowed her eyes and pursed her lips.

Before she could pry for details, Sasha flashed her a smile and swooped in to give her a hug.

"It was so good to see you, but I have to call it a night. I have an early morning meeting."

Bertie squeezed Sasha's shoulders with a surprisingly tight grip.

Sasha abandoned her wine glass and edged her way through the crowd to Connelly.

He was nodding absently as a professorial-looking woman, complete with horn rims and bun, explained the plot of some art house film currently playing in Regent Square.

Sasha touched Connelly's elbow and he glanced down, his mouth curving into a bow when he saw her.

"Pardon, Professor Heckman, let me introduce my wife, Sasha. Sasha, Professor Heckman teaches biology at Chatham University."

"Sylvie Hickman," the woman said, giving Sasha a wide smile and a solid handshake.

"Sasha McCandless ... —Connelly," Sasha said, still tripping over her hyphenated last name a half-year after she'd adopted it. She was glad she'd decided to continue using her maiden name professionally. She'd hate to be so tongue-tied in front of a judge or jury.

"A pleasure."

"I'm sorry to interrupt, but I'm afraid I have to steal my husband before I turn into a pumpkin."

The professor laughed easily and gestured with her empty glass. "Of course. I appear to be in need of a refill, anyway."

Sasha smiled and grabbed Connelly's hand,

guiding him toward the door with the determination of a border collie herding livestock. She dodged clusters of wine lovers and social butterflies, nodding hellos to familiar faces, but didn't stop until they reached the front of the apartment.

"Don't you want to find Daniel and Chris and say our goodbyes?" Connelly asked, as she yanked open the door.

"They'll understand. This place is a madhouse tonight."

He fell into step beside her as they headed along the short hallway to the stairs.

"They know how to throw a party. I guess word gets around," he said.

"I guess so."

"We should have skipped it this week."

She glanced over her shoulder at him as they tromped down the cement stairs. "Why?"

"No reason."

"You know something, don't you? Is it Bricker?" The questions that had been on her lips all day burst out.

Connelly squeezed her hand tight and cut his eyes toward her, pained and wary. "Not here."

They walked in silence the rest of the way home.

Tension followed them into their lobby, up the

stairs, and along the hall to their front door, clinging to them like smoke.

Once inside, Sasha immediately unbuckled the tiny straps on her heels to free her feet from the their four-inch-high prison.

She wiggled her bare toes and sighed in exaggerated relief while Connelly headed straight for the kitchen to feed the cat.

She waited until Java had food and fresh water then she walked around the island and stood directly in front of her husband.

"So? Do you?" she asked.

"Do I have information about Bricker?"

"Yes."

He sighed and leaned back against the counter. His gray eyes were guarded. "Maybe. I don't know."

"Come on."

"Sasha, I can't talk about it. I'm sorry."

She bit down hard on her lip. Took a slow, deep breath. Waited until the urge to shout passed. Then she said, "Is it bad news?"

Connelly shook his head sadly.

"I can't tell you that. I'll tell you this, though—I'm not going to let Bricker hurt you. I promise."

He stepped close and gathered her into his arms.

"I know," she responded, stretching onto her

toes. The reality, of course, was that wasn't a promise he could truly guarantee, and they both knew it.

He bent his head, and covered her mouth with his.

The rest of her questions evaporated, along with her capacity for rational decision-making, and she leaned into his warm chest.

He bent her backwards and scooped her up, headed for the stairs to the bedroom.

And then his phone bleated in his pocket, insistent and shrill.

She knew that ringtone. It was Hank.

She sighed as he deposited her on her feet and fumbled for the phone.

"I'm sorry."

"I know."

They shared a wistful look, then she walked up the stairs to give him some privacy for his call.

She was in the bathroom taking off her jewelry when she heard him jog up the stairs.

She walked to the doorway.

"Can you help me with this clasp?" She gestured toward her necklace.

"Sure."

She turned around and lifted her hair with both hands while he unhooked the tiny spring-ring clasp securing the chain around her neck. His hands were hot against her back as he lifted the necklace. She shivered.

She spun around to face him, and he dropped the chain into her palm, then he scrubbed his face with his hand.

"Uh-oh," she said. "That's not a good sign."

"What's not?"

"That face thing you do. What's wrong?"

"I have to go out."

She stole a glance at the clock.

"Now?"

"Now. I'm sorry."

"When will you be back?"

He shrugged and reknotted his tie. "I don't know. Not tonight. Probably tomorrow evening."

He walked over to the closet and grabbed a bag from the shelves above the clothes bars with one hand and a clean shirt and suit with other.

She wriggled out of her suit dress and hung it on its hanger before throwing on a t-shirt and yoga pants and following him.

He was tossing boxers and socks from his dresser drawer into the bag.

"Can you tell me where you're going?"

"Please don't make me lie to you."

She looked at him for a long moment.

Then she reached over and selected a gray and blue striped tie. "Here. Don't wear the same tie two days in a row. It's gross."

He bent and kissed her then ran a hand over her hair and turned to leave.

She stood there, rooted to the bedroom floor, while he banged around downstairs.

Only after she heard the front door close and the lock engage, did she move.

She trudged down the stairs and bolted the deadbolt.

Her heart was racing. She'd never be able to sleep now. Her eyes swept the too-still, too-quiet condo in search of a distraction and stopped at her laptop resting on the kitchen island.

She powered on the computer and did some stretches while she waited for the machine to boot up. She might as well put her insomnia to productive use.

8

Hank watched as Officer Fornier pawed through yet another stack of files on his gray metal desk.

He did not consider himself an impatient man. He'd spent his youth first on watch duty in the Army, then on stakeouts with the Bureau and, later, on deep undercover assignments with Homeland Security. He knew the value of waiting. And as he'd risen in the ranks, he'd discovered patience was more important than any other attribute he possessed.

But this small-town police officer with his Barney Fife routine was testing him.

"Uh, I'm sorry. I know it's in here somewhere ..." Officer Fornier trailed off.

Hank gritted his teeth.

"Listen, I just need to step out into the hall and make a phone call. You keep looking and I'll be right back, son."

"Will do, sir."

Hank walked out into the institutional corridor, which could have passed for a hallway in any small police station in America and pulled out his phone. He hadn't planned to ask Leo to join him on this visit, mainly because he hadn't wanted to put him in a difficult spot with Sasha. But if Vince Fornier was what passed for local backup, he needed someone reliable. Leo would just have to work out the vagaries of newlywed politics on his own.

As soon as Leo picked up, he rattled off instructions, waited for Leo to confirm his understanding, and then ended the call.

He reentered the messy office hoping against hope that Fornier has made some progress in his search.

But Fornier looked up from under his shaggy bangs—too long for regulation, as far as Hank was concerned—and gave Hank a sheepish shrug. "Sorry."

Hank forced his lips into an approximation of a smile.

"Why don't you just *tell* me what you found instead of looking for your report?" he suggested.

"Tell you?" Fornier blinked.

"You were the responding officer, weren't you, son?"

"Uh, yeah. I mean, yes, sir."

"So, talk me through it. What did you find when you reached the scene? Don't worry about the official report. Once it's loaded up to the national database, I'll be able to access it."

Fornier threw him a panicked look at the mention of the database, but he waved it away.

"We can get someone to walk you through it. It's easy. Just focus on the scene."

The officer cleared his throat and let his eyes drift up toward the ceiling as he recalled the morning's activities.

"It must have been a little before eleven a.m.—um, oh eleven hundred hours, sir—"

Hank cut him off right there. "Just tell it to me like a story, officer. In a conversational way, if you will."

The young patrolman relaxed visibly. He lowered his stiff shoulders and flexed his tensed jaw.

"Sure. Okay. So, it was a little before eleven in the morning. I was out chattin' with Patty, our secretary and dispatcher." He pointed through a narrow doorway to the desk just inside the entrance to the station. "We were tryin' to decide if we should call in an order for lunch at the Pancake Palace. They don't just serve breakfast, you know."

Hank nodded, suddenly regretting the suggestion that the young man tell him a story. "Sure."

"Well, Patty had decided she was gonna go on and eat the salad she packed, when just then the call came in."

"And it was the neighbor who called it in, correct?"

"That's right. Lilah Stokes called it in. Now, you gotta understand that everybody in town knows Lilah is a busybody, and it's been makin' her crazy, the fact that this new family had been living next door since the beginning of last year and she didn't know any of their personal business. And it wasn't for lack of trying—or, more like, prying."

Fornier laughed at his own joke, but he was warming to his story, now, and Hank had no need to prompt him to continue.

"Rightly or wrongly, Patty was rollin' her eyes at Mrs. Stokes' concern. But it was a quiet morning, like most of them are, so I headed over to check it out."

"What exactly did Mrs. Stokes report?"

"She said she was weeding her begonias—that's the flower bed closest to the Bennetts' place." He paused and gave Hank a meaningful look.

"She was spying on her neighbors?" Hank asked.

"Probably."

Hank tried not to grimace at the news that WITSEC had placed a family next door to a nosy neighbor. "Okay, sorry to interrupt. Go on."

"She said she just happened to notice a woman's foot and leg sticking out from behind the sofa. And, before you ask, no, you can't see behind the Bennetts' sofa from her flower bed. At least *I* couldn't, and I have 20/20 vision and about eight inches on Lilah."

"Are you saying she was blatantly peeping in their windows?"

"More or less had to be," Fornier confirmed. "Anyhow, she said she rapped on the window and then rang the doorbell and nobody responded."

"But she didn't hear anything—no fighting or screaming?"

"She says no. She said she'd been shampooing her parlor carpet earlier and that the machine makes a good bit of noise. While the carpet dried, she figured she'd go outside and do som gardening until lunch." He shrugged as if to say *what are you going to do*?

"So no one saw or heard the attack or the attacker?"

"Right."

"And the kids were fishing?"

"Yep. They said they left before sunrise and came back when they got hungry. Thank the Lord they weren't home."

"Amen," Hank replied automatically, although he'd be willing to bet that if they'd been home, there'd have been no attack. He'd bet a tidy sum that Mrs. Stokes hadn't been the only person watching the Bennett house.

"And I told you the rest on the phone. I entered the residence through the unlocked back door and found the victim." He blanched at the memory.

"Bad, huh?" Hank empathized.

Fornier swallowed hard before answering. "I've never seen anything like that before. I mean, we don't have a lot of violent crime in Sunnyvale. I just ... I can't even describe it. Someone really worked her over."

Hank was silent for a moment to let the kid pull himself together.

"Any defensive wounds?"

"The coroner says she probably didn't have

much chance to struggle. He thinks she was running from the guy and tripped over the fringe on her area rug and went down. Most of the blows came after she fell. He probably climbed on top of her and went to town."

"Weapon?"

"Fists. And a garden trowel. Matches the rest of the set in her shed. He used it to bash in her skull."

"Where'd you recover the weapon? Near the body?"

Fornier shook his head. "No. It was weird. It was in the shed right where it belonged. I found it when I checked to make sure the premises were secure. He put it back, but he didn't bother to wipe the blood off it. Who does that?"

A highly disciplined, self-appointed leader who also happens to be a sociopath, Hank thought. He'd be willing to bet a paycheck that Bricker had conditioned his family and followers to always return tools to their designated spot after use.

"The shed was unlocked?" he asked.

"No lock on it."

"And you checked the house top to bottom?"

"Yeah. I swept the first floor before I called the body in. I had to wait until the coroner came out to bag her to do a more thorough search of the property. I was pretty busy trying to keep the oldest boy out of the house."

The boy.

"Let's talk about the boy. What exactly did he say when he asked you to call me?"

Hank had to assume the kid had been in a panic and had blurted out that the family was in the witness protection program.

The officer scrunched his face up and thought. "Let's see. He got rid of the sister. He sent her to put the fishing equipment away—"

"In the shed?" Hank wanted to know.

"Yeah, as a matter of fact."

"She didn't notice the trowel?"

"Apparently not. It was pretty dark in there. It looked like she hung up the rods, dumped the rest of the gear, and rolled. The fishing equipment was along the back wall. The gardening tools were all arranged on a potting bench in one corner. Why?"

"Just trying to picture it, son. Go on."

"Once she walked away, he got this stony look on his face like he was trying to man up. He asked if his mom was dead and before I could answer, he pulled out your card and said if I thought she was murdered I needed to call you."

Hank considered this piece of information.

"And that's what I did," Fornier said.

"Who else have you reported this to?"

Fornier shot him a confused look. "No one. Who else would I report it to?"

"Well, your chief, for one?"

"Sure, ordinarily. I didn't, though, because he's out of town."

"Business or pleasure?"

"Uh, vacation. I haven't bothered him. Should I?"

"Not yet," Hank said.

He tried to hide his excitement. If WITSEC had bothered to tell anyone in Sunnyvale that they'd placed a witness there, it would have been the local chief of police. Who would have been sworn to secrecy. So if Fornier didn't know—and he didn't appear to—and he delayed telling his chief, Hank could just maybe get a handle on the situation before WITSEC even learned about Anna Bennett's death.

"So, that's pretty much it." Fornier shuffled from side to side and tried not to make it obvious that he was looking at the wall clock.

"Your shift ended a while ago didn't it, son?"

"About two hours, sir. But I'm in no hurry," the kid lied.

"You've had a rough day, Officer Fornier. I'm going to turn in for the night, myself. You should go home and kiss your wife if you have one. We'll pick it back up in the morning," Hank lied right back to him.

"Yes, sir. Do you need directions to the hotel?"

Fornier was packing up his duffle bag as he spoke.

"I'm all set. Thanks."

They walked out together. Fornier paused to say good night to his replacement, who was lurking around the reception area waiting for them to finish up and get out of his office.

Hank stepped up his pace. No need for the kid to see him driving the opposite direction from the hotel and start asking himself questions.

"I'M on my way to the airport now. I'll be there as soon as I can," Leo said. He couldn't remember ever hearing Hank so agitated.

"That's not soon enough." Hank's voice boomed through the Bluetooth connection.

Leo checked his speed. Seventy miles an hour was about as fast as he was willing to drive through Downtown Pittsburgh, even if it was deserted at this hour.

"Why don't you fill me in while I'm en route?" he suggested.

"I'm a little busy at the moment. There are six of them, remember? They were eating dinner when I got here, but now they're all wound up and they won't go to bed."

Despite himself, Leo grinned—Hank's sense of urgency was beginning to make sense. Here was a man who had walked right into a rumored al Qaeda safe house without waiting for backup, but leave him alone with six kids for a couple of hours and he was already cracking.

"I could have brought Sasha. Then we'd only have been outnumbered two to one."

Hank's voice grew serious. "You didn't tell her. Tell me you didn't tell her."

"Relax. I didn't tell her. I still don't agree with the decision, but we can fight it out later—after the half-dozen criminal masterminds wear down your defenses."

In the background, he could hear a girl squealing. "Piggyback, Uncle Hank!"

"I have to go," Hank said. "Just hurry."

"Sure thing, Uncle Hank."

Hank disconnected the call, and Leo laughed aloud at the image of Hank cavorting around in a dark suit and a tie with a freckle-faced kid clinging to his neck.

The laughter was short-lived, though, because Hank and the Bennett kids were in a dangerous situation. If the local police were as inept as Hank had claimed when he'd ordered Leo to fly down, then Hank really was an army of one. Which was fine if Bricker had slunk back into the ooze, content to have gotten his revenge on the woman who helped convict him.

But trying to tease out the motivation of a madman was, itself, an exercise in madness. Bricker could be lurking somewhere nearby, preparing to strike again.

Hank's decision to sit on the kids himself was valiant, but it was no kind of plan.

And Leo was a man who liked to have a plan.

He switched on the classic rock station, turning the volume way up to drown out his thoughts. He pressed his foot against the gas pedal and rocketed across the Fort Pitt Bridge, leaving the city behind.

9

It was close to eleven o'clock when Leo nosed his rental vehicle into the Bennetts' driveway. Every other house on the block was dark, the blinds drawn and the exterior lights extinguished for the night. The Bennett house was the sole exception. Lights blazed from every window.

As he neared the front door, he could hear the babble of kids' voices.

He gave the doorbell a short jab and waited.

After a moment, Hank's silhouette filled the doorway. A porch light flickered to life, and Leo shielded his eyes with his hand.

The door swung open.

"Took you long enough."

"My trip was fine. Thanks for asking," Leo said, edging past Hank and into the hallway.

Hank pushed the door shut and secured the deadbolt.

Leo started toward the back of the house, where he could hear kids jabbering and laughing. Hank put out a hand and yanked him back by his arm.

"Wait. Let me fill you in on the situation," Hank said in a low rumbling voice.

Leo stopped. "Okay."

"When I got here, they seemed to be holding up pretty well. But I think the shock's wearing off and they're starting to really understand that Mom's not coming home, ever. The little ones get worked up off and on. One of them will start to cry for mommy, and it has a domino effect. The oldest two are pretty good at calming everyone down, but I see in their faces that the reality is hitting them now, too. And the middle ones are scared, just straight-up terrified. I rented some Pixar movie online and let them eat a bag of chocolate chips, but I'm out of ideas."

"They probably need to talk to someone—a counselor or something."

"I guess so. If there even are any in this weak

excuse for a town." Hank jerked his hands through his short hair.

"Why are we staying here, anyway?"

Hank stared at him.

"Where else do you want to go?"

"Anywhere. Look, if WITSEC has a leak, this place is compromised. If there's no leak, it's still best practice to leave because, well, it's compromised anyway."

Hank nodded. "Procedure would be to move them."

"Right. And I had time to think about it on the plane. We have the luxury of not following strict procedure. We don't have to relocate them for good. We just need to get them out of here."

"Tomorrow. Or the next day. At least let them get a good night's sleep. They just lost their mom, they don't need any more trauma right now."

"You're the one who said the locals are useless. Why stay here? We're sitting ducks."

"I hear you. We'll move out in the morning." Hank's tone was final.

A wail—either of sorrow or fury—rose from the kitchen, followed by an explosion of kids shouting over one another. Leo bit back his futile retort and headed for the kitchen.

Hank trailed him.

At the sight of two large men hulking in the doorway, the furor in the kitchen stopped, as if someone had hit pause.

Hank hung back and let Leo go first.

He squinted as he entered the large, bright kitchen. Every overhead light was switched on. In contrast, the family room just to the right, where their mother's body had been found, was dark and silent. It didn't take a degree in child psychology to figure out what was going on.

The Bennetts were crowded around the kitchen island. The oldest boy and girl each held a little one on a lap. The middle two kids had pulled their stools close and were sitting shoulder to shoulder. All six faces reflected varying degrees of worry, confusion, grief, shock, sorrow, fear—emotions that had no business haunting children.

Especially not these children, who'd already been uprooted from their lives and betrayed by their father.

Leo's chest squeezed. He knew that feeling. Not like the Bennett kids, to be sure, but he knew the heavy loneliness of being fatherless in a strange place.

He cleared his throat.

"Hi, I'm Leo." He smiled encouragingly at the

littlest boy, who popped a thumb into his mouth and looked back at Leo with serious eyes.

The girl who was holding the boy answered. "I'm Be—Brianna."

"I remember you," Leo told her. She and the boy, now known as Cole, had kept it together long enough to hustle their siblings out of harm's way before Sasha and Leo had stormed her father's armed compound.

She smiled uncertainly.

The little girl looked up from Cole's lap. "You're Cousin Leo?"

Sure, why not? If they could have an African-American Uncle Hank, they may as well have a half-Vietnamese Cousin Leo.

"Yep, that's me, Cousin Leo." He winked at her and was rewarded with a giggle.

Her laughter faded quickly.

"So what's the plan?" Cole asked in a dull, tired voice.

"I know you all have had a heck of a day. And I want you to know we're all really sorry about your mom. But Hank and I are going to take you somewhere safe in the morning, okay? Let's try to get some sleep." He kept his voice soft.

Tears welled up in the middle boy's eyes, who wiped them away with the back of his hand.

"We have to leave?" Leah, the one who used to be named Lacey, asked. Her lip trembled.

"Just for a little while."

"Where?" the middle boy, Mark, asked.

"Back up North," Leo said, which was about as much detail as he could provide, seeing as how he had no idea where they were going.

He turned toward Brianna and Cole and tried to decide how to broach the subject of go-bags. He assumed their mother hadn't shed all of her old habits. "Do you have bags packed already? You know—just in case?"

Brianna shook her head. "Mom said we didn't need to do that anymore." Her voice dropped and she stared down at her feet.

"Oh. Well, in the morning you should each grab a backpack and fill it with a couple outfits, a pair of pajamas, and your toiletries. And, uh, everyone go ahead and think about a special toy or book or something you want to bring. Okay?"

He looked around the island and was met by six nodding heads.

"Great. Now, it's really late. Let's make it a race against the clock to get ready for bed. See how fast you can do it."

They jumped off the stools and started running for the stairs.

"Wait," Brianna said, skidding to a stop near the refrigerator.

Cole stopped beside her. "What's up?"

"The ice envelope."

"Ice envelope?" Leo parroted.

Cole shook his head in self-disgust. "How could we forget?"

The girl pulled open the freezer door and shifted bags of frozen vegetables and packages of meat until she a located a letter-sized manila envelope.

"ICE. In Case of Emergency. Mom always kept the ICE envelope in the freezer. You know, with the ice," she explained to Leo with a tremulous smile.

"Sure."

She handed the envelope to her brother, and they stared down at it together. Leo looked over Cole's shoulder. "OPEN ICE" was printed across the front of the envelope in neat, feminine lettering. But that isn't what caused Leo's heart to thump in his chest. Clipped to the front of the envelope was a cream-colored business card with distinctive navy blue lettering. He leaned forward and peered at the words to confirm what he already knew: Sasha's business card was in the dead woman's freezer.

10

Tuesday

Sasha gulped her coffee as she hurried along South Highland Avenue toward her office.

Her late-night work session had allowed her to catch up on her caseload but it had come at a cost. She was exhausted.

Of course, that wasn't all due to the hours spent researching the available remedies for a breached contract to build a retail space to suit. The nightmares had contributed, too.

It was always the same story, even though the

details changed. She dreamed about Bricker, out there, getting closer. He was coming for her.

She balled her hand into a fist then released it. To her surprise, her primary emotion wasn't fear, it was anger. She *wanted* to face Bricker.

She was looking forward to being there when he was captured and dragged away in handcuffs. Bricker had killed her friend. He'd crashed her wedding. To the agents who were spread out across the country searching for him, he was a faceless danger—the larger-than-life mastermind who'd nearly succeeded in starting a pandemic and who'd managed to escape from a federal prison. But to her, he was a very specific, very personal threat: And she was going to kick his ass.

Her heart rate was rising. She checked her calendar. No meetings until after lunch.

Good. She'd call Daniel and see if he could squeeze in a sparring session at noon. She had some aggression to work out.

She took another swig of coffee and gagged. Was there anything grosser than cold coffee?

She charged into the building and beelined for Jake's coffee shop for a fresh, hot coffee.

Jake waved good morning on his way through to the kitchen as she joined the short line at the coffee bar. It was a little early for Jake's usual clientele, herself excepted.

The new guy at the counter greeted her with a grin and two fresh mugs of coffee.

"Nicaraguan dark, right?"

"Thanks. I see my reputation precedes me, but I don't usually double-fist coffees."

He laughed. "I figured your friend could use a warm up."

She stared at him blankly.

"You know, your friend with the crazy eyes? She was waiting here when I opened. She said something about having a Property exam tonight." He jerked his head to the doorway.

"Oh, right. Thanks."

She scooped up the mugs and headed for Naya's office.

Out of hands, she rapped on the door with her foot.

"Come in," Naya called.

"Open the door. I come bearing caffeine," she shouted back.

The door opened inward, and a smiling Naya appeared in the doorway.

She grabbed one of the mugs from Sasha's hands.

"Awesome. Thank you!" She spoke rapid-fire

and too loud, like someone who had had far too little sleep and far too much coffee.

"You're in a good mood for someone who has a Property final looming on the horizon," Sasha said as she eyed the mug, wondering if she should try to ease it out of Naya's hand.

Naya seemed to sense her plan and gripped the handle more tightly.

"The hard exams are behind me now. Property's a breeze. Home stretch, baby, hoooooome stretch!"

Sasha swallowed her skepticism. Different strokes, and all, but she didn't recall there being anything particularly easy about the rule against perpetuities, vested remainders, and conditions precedent.

"Whatever gets you through."

"Right. Hey, you and Fly Boy want to grab a bite with me and Carl after my exam? I could use a little break."

At the mention of Connelly, Sasha felt herself stiffen.

"He's out of town, but I could meet you guys for a late dinner—unless you'd rather just make it a date. I'm sure Carl hasn't seen much of you lately."

Naya rolled her eyes. "No, he hasn't. And he's been moaning like a baby about it. I was hoping Leo could provide some perspective on being with a powerful career woman. Where is he, anyway?"

"I don't know."

Naya's eyes widened

"What do you mean you don't know?"

"I told you yesterday. He's not telling me everything."

Worry flashed across Naya's face. "Do you think it's Bricker?"

"Maybe. Don't worry about it. I'll get it out of him eventually. You focus on exams. Talk to Carl and let me know about dinner, but I think you should just give him some one-on-one attention tonight." She winked. "That's my advice, from powerful career woman to powerful career woman."

Naya laughed. "Yeah, you're probably right. Rain check on dinner?"

"You know it."

Sasha turned to leave.

"Hey, Mac—"

"What?"

"You should call Aroostine. If something's going on with Bricker, she ought to know."

11

"I'm sorry I can't help you, but I'm still *persona non grata* at Justice. No one's telling me anything."

Aroostine's frustration was palpable through the phone line.

Sasha clucked her tongue sympathetically. "You'll be back in the saddle soon."

It had taken her the better part of the day to catch up with Aroostine, and after all that phone tag, it turned out she was just as in the dark as Sasha was—maybe more.

Aroostine had been unfairly demoted from a plum spot in the Criminal Division of the Department of Justice to a field position with the U.S. Attorney General's Office in Johnstown, Pennsylvania.

Her mistake? Missing jury selection to save the lives of two innocent people and thwart an international criminal's efforts to control vulnerable and sensitive national information. But, rules are rules, and her boss had shipped her off to the hinterlands in a snit.

"I don't really care if I ever get back to headquarters. Honestly, I'm happier back home with Joe and out in the community working with local law enforcement. D.C. was a hornet's nest. But I do care that they're freezing me out of the Bricker investigation."

Sasha found herself nodding even though Aroostine couldn't see her. Aroostine was within her rights to be angry. She'd been part of the original criminal investigation into Jeffrey Bricker and his prepper group, and she'd been held hostage by Bricker's mercenaries at Sasha and Connelly's wedding. She had her own reasons to want to see Bricker back behind bars.

"I'm glad you're happy in Johnstown, at least."

"Thanks. Listen, for all the good it'll do, I'll send some feelers out. Are you concerned about something in particular or are you just interested in a general status?"

Sasha hesitated.

"Uh, just a general status. But listen, don't do anything that's going to get you in trouble."

Aroostine laughed dryly. "How much more trouble could I get into?"

"I don't know, are there any crappier U.S. Attorney postings vacant?"

They laughed together for a moment, then something caught Sasha's eye out her window. A passenger van pulled into a spot across the street and Connelly got out of the driver's seat. He waited for a teenage boy to join him from the rear of the van. They dodged the late afternoon traffic and darted across the street toward her building.

"Hey, I gotta go. I'll talk to you soon."

She ended the call and waited for Connelly and the kid to show up in her office. She didn't have long to wait.

The sound of heavy footsteps falling along the outside corridor announced their arrival, followed by two short raps on her half-open door.

Connelly stuck his head into the office without waiting for her to call out an invitation.

"Hey, do you have a minute?"

He looked worse than she felt—pale and tired, with dark half-rings under his bleary eyes.

"Hey yourself. Come on in."

He pushed the door open and walked into the office followed by the teenage boy.

She put the boy's age at about sixteen, maybe a little older. He was tall and lanky. He had pale, freckled skin. She couldn't see his eyes because his gaze was fixed on the floor just ahead of his feet, and his light brown hair hung over his forehead.

Something about the way he carried himself was familiar, though.

Connelly reached behind him and pulled her door shut.

"You remember Clay Bricker, don't you, Sasha?" he asked.

At the sound of his name, the boy jerked his head up, eyes flashing. "It's Cole Bennett now."

Of course. The oldest Bricker boy—the one who'd driven Gavin Russell's car to get his siblings out of the compound and to safety.

She smiled brightly and stuck out her hand, "Of course. What a wonderful surprise to see you again, Cole."

He blinked at her. "You don't know?"

She glanced at Connelly, who was studiously staring over her head out the window, and then back at the boy. "Pardon?"

"My mom's been murd—she's dead," he choked out the words.

Her stomach seized. It felt for all the world as if Daniel had just landed a reverse punch to her core. Blood rushed to her head, making it impossible to think. She was hot. Her ears buzzed. She shook her head as if she could reject the words and make them untrue.

But, of course, they were true. The boy's pain was stretched across his face.

"What?! When? Oh my God."

Cole stared at her mutely while she tried to process what he'd said. Connelly came over and stood very close to her.

He spoke in a low, urgent murmur. "I'm sorry. I couldn't tell you. I promise I'll bring you up to speed later, but right now Cole needs you."

She bit down hard on her lower lip until she managed to craft an answer she wouldn't regret.

"We need to have a serious talk after this."

"I know."

She exhaled shakily and raised her eyes to his. "Bricker?"

He gave her a look beyond description—tender, frightened, resolved. Finally he said, "Officially, we don't know. But ..."

He trailed off, and she nodded. Of course it was Bricker. She waited out the frisson of fear that coursed through her veins and then turned back to Cole.

"I'm so sorry. What can I do?"

Both the sorrow and the question were genuine. She had no idea how she could help Cole, but presumably he wouldn't be standing in her office unless Connelly had a plan.

"A lot," Connelly said. "Let's sit down and talk."

"Oh, right. Sorry. Please, Cole, have a seat. Do you guys want some ... drinks?"

She'd been about to offer them coffee but tripped over the word. Was it okay to offer a teenager coffee? Her grandmother had started sneaking it to her when she was twelve, but her mother insisted it had stunted her growth. Cole looked to be pretty close to fully grown.

Connelly shot her a look like he knew what she was thinking. "We're fine."

They lowered themselves into her guest chairs stiffly.

She was struck by a sudden thought.

"Wait, so where's Hank?" she asked. "And the rest of the kids."

The boy rolled his eyes. Connelly jerked a thumb toward the window.

"They're in the van, and Uncle Hank is getting antsy. He's working the phone trying to find us a safe house, but there's a lot of ... background noise."

"It's like being trapped in a snare drum with a wildcat," Cole deadpanned in a creditable imitation of Hank's rumbling baritone.

Sasha almost laughed but then recalled the reason for their visit.

"So, what can I do for you, Cole?"

"I don't know, but you must. My mom sent us," Cole blurted, apparently out of patience for small talk.

"Your mom?" she repeated, certain she'd misheard him.

"Yes," he said thickly, digging his hand into his pocket.

She glanced at Connelly, who raised his eyebrows and gave a slight nod of confirmation.

A dead woman sent them?

Cole thrust a crumpled card at her.

"What's this?" she asked as she reached for it.

"Your business card. Anna—I mean—Allison Bennett had it clipped to the front of an envelope that she kept in the freezer." Connelly answered.

She stared down at the card in her hand. It was definitely hers. That was her name--Sasha McCandless, Esquire. And beneath that, her title: Partner, McCandless & Volmer. That was the distinctive orange stripe that Will had wanted to add to the card.

She blinked and looked up, meeting Connelly's eyes.

"Did you give it to her that night at the compound?"

Sasha shook her head. "No."

"Maybe later, during the trial?"

"No," she repeated, clearing her throat.

Connelly and Cole watched her, waiting.

"I didn't give this card to your mother," she told the boy.

"Sure you did. She must have thought you'd help us if something happened," he insisted.

"I hope she thought that," Sasha said slowly. "And I hope I can. But this card is new. We had them printed after Will left Prescott last summer," she continued, addressing Connelly more than the kid now. "The first orders didn't even have this orange bar." She pointed at the design.

"When did you add that?" Connelly asked.

She searched her memory. "Right before we left for the wedding. There was a full box waiting on my desk when we got back from the honeymoon. I don't know how she got this."

"Who cares how she got it?" Cole snapped. "Are you going to help me or not?"

"Of course I am," she soothed. She turned the card in her fingers. "What do you need."

Cole floundered. "I don't know. Here. This is my mom's ICE envelope." He pulled a thick manila envelope from his back pocket. It had been rolled lengthwise into a tube.

"Ice?"

"In Case of Emergency," Connelly explained.

She took the envelope and smoothed it out to examine the front. 'Open ICE" was printed across the front in thick black marker. The printing was neat, sure—the hand of a mother planning for contingencies, keeping order in her home.

"Your card was attached right there on the corner," Connelly said.

"And this was in the freezer?"

"Freezer's better than a safe. Secure in the event of a fire. Not attractive to roving bands of thieves. Easily accessible. Hide it in the open, or at least in among the frozen peas," Cole recited.

"Did your dad teach you that?" she asked before she could stop herself.

Cole barked out a short laugh. "Him? No. He was all about safes. The bigger and stronger the better. Titanium, retina scans, whatever. No, the freezer thing was all Mom."

It was a clever spot to use. She gave him a wan smile.

"May I open it?"

"That's the idea. It's full of papers, but they're all legal mumbo-jumbo," Cole said.

She worked the clasp and slid out a sheaf of documents. She flipped through them, *Last Will and Testament of Allison Bennett, Financial Power of Attorney, Health Care Power of Attorney, Irrevocable Trust for the Benefit of the Bennett Children, Appointment of Trustee.*

She looked up at Connelly. "This is a lot of reading material. Let me make a copy of all this stuff and start working through it. Why don't you rescue Hank? I'm sure the kids are hungry and bored. Go get something to eat. I'll call your cell."

"Are you sure?"

"I'm sure."

He stood, and Cole followed suit.

"Thank you, Ms. McCandless. I mean, Mrs. Connelly?"

"Call me Sasha."

Connelly walked over and kissed her softly. "Mrs. Connelly sounds better, you know."

She arched a brow at that.

"Go on. Get out of here and let me do my thing."

12

Bricker made it from Sunnyvale all the way up to Weirton, West Virginia along the network, handed off from one conductor to another. But at a rundown McDonald's just south of Weirton, the system broke down.

Pete, the red-hatted truck driver who'd picked him up in Norfolk, shrugged apologetically and kicked at the gravel with the toe of his boot as he broke the news. "Looks like your next conductor's a no-show, Captain."

"Did something happen?" he demanded, worried that the government had somehow gotten wind of the railroad system or, worse yet, his movements.

"Uh-yup." Pete aimed a stream of chewing tobacco at the weeds growing alongside the parking lot. "He got his self picked up on a drug charge, according to the local contact. They're looking for a replacement now, sir. I'm sorry I can't take you further down the road. I've got to get back. I'm driving a long haul run. I head out to Iowa tomorrow."

Bricker realized he'd been holding his breath. He exhaled in relief and offered Pete a firm handshake.

"Of course, of course. No apologies necessary. Thank you for your service."

Although he no longer held an official leadership position as the head of Preppers PA, he remained a legend within the movement. The men who risked their security to help him deserved his respect.

Pete bobbed his head and jerked a thumb around toward the back of the McDonald's.

"Don't mention it, sir. Guy in the kitchen is going to help you out. Knock on the back door and ask for T-Bone."

"T-Bone?"

"Yup. 'Fraid so."

"We trust this man?" Bricker asked.

Pete cleared his throat and answered slowly. "I don't know him myself. Can't vouch for him, but the local guys say he's been coming around and seems eager and able."

Bricker kept his face a neutral mask. "I see. Thanks again for the lift."

Pete nodded and headed back to his pickup while Bricker squared his shoulders and trudged past the Dumpsters to the back of the restaurant. He rapped on the windowless steel door. While he waited, he swiveled his head from side to side, constantly scanning for passersby.

After a moment, a scrawny guy pushed the door open and looked around the parking lot, wild-eyed. He had a shaved head, and blue-inked tattoos peeked out from the neck of his polyester uniform shirt.

"Are you T-Bone?" Bricker asked, ignoring his misgivings.

Young men like this were punks, dancing on the fringes of neo-Nazism, incarceration, and drug abuse. They were attention-seekers and, as far as he was concerned, they represented a weak link within the larger movement.

But at the moment, T-Bone was his lifeline.

"That's me. Here you go, Captain Bricker, I'm sure you're hungry." He shoved a grease-stained bag of food into Bricker's hands.

"Thank you, son."

The young man smiled and his pronounced Adam's apple bobbed.

"I can't let you in the back but when my shift ends, I can drive you as far as Bridgeville," he whispered.

His eyes shifted from Bricker's face to the scraggly trees at the edge of the lot behind him. "Maybe you can wait in the woods?"

Bricker raised an eyebrow at the classification of the patch of dirt as woods. The sad trees lining the lot provided no cover.

"I'll find a spot to hunker down. When does your shift end?"

"About two more hours. If things slow down and the manager asks for volunteers to punch out early, I'll jump on it."

"Two hours is fine." Bricker turned toward the brush then turned back. "Wait. Where exactly is Bridgeville?"

"Uh, just south of Pittsburgh?" The kid answered with a question in his own voice. "Maybe thirty minutes or so outside the city."

Bricker nodded a goodbye.

He walked into the trees clutching his bag of fried food. He didn't bother to hide his smile.

Just outside the city? He'd be within striking distance of Sasha McCandless by morning. He'd have to scout a suitable hiding spot to use as a base and then get a handle on the lawyer's routines. He was eager to strike, but he had to proceed with maximum caution, especially in light of the government agents and other law enforcement types who apparently followed McCandless around like puppy dogs. According to the team he'd hired to storm her wedding, they hadn't been prepared for guests who would resist and fight back. Well, he didn't intend to make that mistake.

Killing Anna had fueled him to wrap up the rest of the loose ends faster. He had to take care of the lawyer and her husband and, if he got in the way, their good pal Richardson. Once he'd evened the score with them, he could turn to the final piece of business—getting his children out of the clutches of the federal government.

Anger flared in his belly and a red mist clouded his vision. The idea of the corrupt, inept government enslaving *his* children was what had fueled him during his imprisonment. Their mother's shameful complicity aside, he hadn't raised his children to submit to the will of a bunch of craven bureaucrats.

His last attempt to force the government to its knees had failed because he'd had to rely on others. This time, he was going to do it alone. A single man, driven to free his children from their government yoke. No holds would be barred. If he went down in a blaze of gunfire, like the true patriots who'd gone before him at places like Ruby Ridge, then so be it.

He plowed through the jagged brush at the edge of the lot and pushed his way through the long weeds. He had to sacrifice quiet for speed in order to put some distance between himself and the row of fast food restaurants.

Once he could no longer hear the rush of traffic on the highway, he slowed his pace and began to search for an adequate spot to stop. He crouched under a canopy of vines, tore open the bag, and wolfed down the burger. Then he crumpled the bag into a ball and shoved it in his pocket. *Leave no trace.*

He sat under the vines and waited for time to pass, jittering his leg to release his pent up energy.

First, McCandless.

Then his children.

13

"I gave it to her," Naya said.

She closed her outline and set her highlighter on her desk then looked up at Sasha with a stricken look.

Sasha pocketed the business card.

"It's okay."

"I didn't know it was her, Mac." Her voice shook.

"Well, of course you didn't. It's *okay*."

"A woman called the office right after New Year's Day. She said her resolution was to get her affairs in order. We got a bunch of calls like that in early January, actually."

"Sure."

It made sense. Procrastinating about having a will prepared was a national pastime, but overcoming inertia was relatively easy: Call a lawyer and get the ball rolling and then turn to more painful pursuits like giving up sugar or training for a marathon.

"I told her—I tell all of them that we don't do that. I explain that you and Will are trial lawyers, but I offer to give them referrals."

"Allison Bennett took down the name I gave her but she asked me to send her your card, just in case she needed it for something else. I remember because she gave me her address. I told her you're not admitted to practice in North Carolina and that she should get a local attorney for her estate work, anyway."

Sasha nodded. "Good answer."

"But she said she had ties to Pennsylvania and needed an attorney up here, too. Anyway, I sent her a set of the marketing materials Will had printed up and one of your cards." Naya placed her palms flat on the desk as if she were bracing herself. "Did I lead Bricker to her?"

The truth, of course, was Sasha had no idea. But the notion that Bricker had access to the firm's mailing list database sent a shiver up her spine. And Naya looked sick, like she might vomit all over her exam preparation materials. So Sasha did the only thing she could do. She lied.

"Absolutely not. The feds are working all the angles. Don't you think they'd be crawling all over this place and pissing you off while you try to study if they thought for a minute Bricker found her through us?"

The color returned to Naya's face. "But seriously, get back to work. I have what I need."

She was glad to have closed the loop on how her business card had gotten into Allison's hands, but she had to get back to work herself. Her eyes had started to glaze over about two paragraphs into her reading of Allison's will. She'd gone hunting for answers on the card in an effort to wake herself up as much as to find an answer.

"Thanks for talking me down, Mac."

"It's what I do." She turned to leave and then had a thought. "Hey, did you give her a recommendation for an estates and trust lawyer?"

Naya narrowed her eyes for a moment and thought. "I sure did."

Sasha waited.

"Marshall Alverson."

Sasha blinked. "You sent her to Prescott?"

Naya had the decency to look sheepish. "Listen, I usually refer people to Kevin Williams, over in the Lawyers' Building, for simple wills. But she said she had some complicated issues. Complicated issues, large amounts of money—those things call for a specialist. And where are you gonna find a specialist? It's either P&T or WC&C." She raised an eyebrow. "And say what you will about our former employer, but they're less dodgy than Whitmore, Clay, & Charles."

Sasha matched her with a raised brow of her own. "The less dodgy of the two dodgiest, stodgiest firms in town? That's quite an endorsement. Did he take her on as a client, do you know?"

"How would I know? Those fools don't even bother to say 'thanks.' They *assume* a steady flow of clients is a God-given right. Meanwhile, Kevin sends me a gift card every time I send him a client."

Sasha left her stewing in her annoyance with Prescott & Talbott's entitlement attitude.

SASHA ADDED the Health Care Power of Attorney to the growing pile of documents to her left and stifled a yawn.

She glanced at the dwindling pile to her right. All she had left was Allison's Irrevocable Trust and the Appointment of Trustee and then she could claim her treat.

Espresso. She could almost taste it.

And not a quick run to Jake's for his pitiful excuse for espresso. As her reward for numbing her eyeballs, not to mention her brain, with page after page of stilted, convoluted language that no lawyer had spoken since the eighteen hundreds, she'd earned the real deal.

She was going to take a trip to the intimidating, fancy espresso bar downtown. She might even get one of their dense dark chocolate, caramel, and sea salt bars, known to the rest of the world by the less esoteric name of 'brownie.' She wasn't a sweets lover, but she made an exception for those bars.

The promise of the nirvana that awaited her propelled her forward. She plucked the trust document from the table and started reading. She made it almost all the way through the first sentence before she had her first question. The document was styled an *"irrevocable testamentary trust for the benefit of the minor children of Allison Bennett."*

She dialed Will's extension.

"Yes? Is Naya rampaging?"

She chuckled. "Not to my knowledge. Do you have a minute?"

"Always."

"I'll be right down."

She ended the call and swept her documents into her arms. She trotted down the short hallway to Will's office. His door was open, so she walked right in and plopped herself into his guest chair.

"Aren't all testamentary trusts, by definition, irrevocable?" she asked without preamble.

Will made a contemplative noise. She recognized it as his professorial warm up.

"Well, with the caveat that this obviously is not my area of expertise, I'd say that's correct. The difference between a revocable trust and an irrevocable trust is that the latter cannot be changed by the grantor once it takes effect."

"And a testamentary trust doesn't take effect until the grantor dies, right?"

"Correct. And, obviously, unless there've been some advances in science that I don't know about, a dead grantor can't make any changes."

That all squared with what she thought.

"Then can you think of any reason why an attorney would draft a testamentary trust to specify that it's irrevocable?"

He scratched his chin.

"Hmm. Possibly just out of an abundance of caution. Maybe the drafter is a belt and suspenders type."

Of course.

If there was one hallmark of Prescott & Talbott's transactional attorneys, it was their insistence on building redundancies into their documents. It used to drive her nuts when she'd have to go to trial over a document that had been inelegantly drafted to provide the ultimate in butt-covering for the attorney, invariably at the expense of clarity and unambiguity. The trial lawyers all rolled their eyes at the belts-and-suspenders approach their colleagues favored when everyone knew that either/or would keep your pants up.

"Right. That makes sense. Hey, if you had a thorny estate issue, who would you refer it out to?"

"Marsh Alverson, without a doubt." Will answered confidently and without hesitation.

"Great. Thanks."

"Wait. Are you doing a will? I don't know if our malpractice carrier would approve. Not that you aren't competent, of course. It's just somewhat far afield of your expertise, don't you think?"

Behind his glasses, his eyes flashed with concern.

"No, don't worry. The estate I'm asking about has already been farmed out—to your pal at Prescott, as it happens."

"Oh? Is it in dispute now?"

She hesitated, chewing on her lower lip while she thought. Finally she decided she owed her law partner an explanation. After all, she'd agreed to represent the Bennett children's interests. Her representation affected the firm and, hence, Will. He needed to be in the loop. Connelly and Hank didn't have to like it, but they'd just have to deal with it.

"Not exactly. The decedent's heirs asked me to represent them, though. It looks like it could get hairy. Our clients are the six minor children of a woman who was just murdered."

He rocked back in his seat.

"Good Lord. Do the authorities have a suspect?"

"I'm not sure about the authorities, but Hank and Connelly seem to think Bricker killed her."

"*Jeffrey* Bricker? The prepper Bricker?"

"That's the one. It's his wife, Will. Anna Bricker's dead. And she left my contact information for her kids with her estate papers."

Complete silence stretched across his office.

She waited a long minute. Then she said, "Will?"

"This is a serious development." Will's voice lacked its usual reassuring timbre. He sounded squeaky and unsure. In truth, he sounded scared.

"It is. And I have no more information, because Connelly and Hank haven't told me anything. They think they're protecting us by keeping us in the dark. Why don't you see if you can get anything out of our favorite shadow agents while I wade through this trust language?"

Will huffed.

"Listen," she continued, "I'm not just putting you off. Believe me. I'm almost as in the dark as you are. But I need to review these documents."

And get my espresso, she added silently.

"Well ... fine. Are the children safe?"

She braced herself in anticipation of his reaction.

"Probably as safe as they can possibly be. They're with Connelly and Hank."

"What?!"

"Will, please. I need to turn to Anna's—er, Allison's—estate issues."

"Of course. I'm sorry. But did you say Allison?"

"She changed her name to Allison Bennett."

"Of course."

She leaned forward and gave him an earnest look.

"I'm as irritated as you are with all the secrecy, Will."

He sighed. "I know. Not to defend them, but for all their cowboy ways, Leo and Hank *are* dyed-in-wool feds. It doesn't come naturally for them to share information."

"Right. DNTK."

"Pardon?"

"Oh, it's Connelly's favorite answer to just about any request for information—demonstrate need to know."

Will nodded thoughtfully. "I can see that. Okay, you immerse yourself in your estates and trust work. I'll take care of the other."

"Thanks, Will."

She hauled herself back to her office and resumed her tedious reading. She only made it through one additional paragraph before she saw something that literally stopped her heart for a brief moment. The section appointing the trustee of the irrevocable testamentary trust provided that said trustee was to be one *Sasha McCandless-Connelly, Esquire.*

14

"Do you want another shot?"

Marsh gestured at her empty espresso cup.

Yes. Oh, so very much.

"No thanks."

"You sure?"

"Well, maybe a latte." She figured adding some milk to the next cup of coffee would be prudent. And she figured Marshall Alverson, Belt-and-Suspenders Attorney-at-Law, owed her at least one more caffeinated beverage. Maybe also something more valuable—say, a kidney.

"Be right back."

He popped up from the table and beelined toward the front counter.

Marsh scurried back to the table with an oversized mug, steam rising from the milk.

"Thanks," she said as he placed it in front of her.

"My pleasure."

She took a sip then sat the mug down. "So. Let's get down to business, shall we? You seem oddly incurious about why I invited you for coffee."

"I assumed it was just, you know, networking. Your office has sent us some work. I thought, perhaps you wanted to build camaraderie."

"Really? I left Prescott before you joined the firm. You assumed I just wanted to have a collegial coffee break with a total stranger? It didn't occur to you—" she lowered her voice to a hiss—"that it might have something to do with the fact that you drafted a trust naming me as trustee for six minors and never bothered to ask me if I wanted to serve?"

The color drained from his face. He picked up his cup and took a long drink, obviously buying time.

"Not really, to be honest. I couldn't very well tell you Ms. Bennett had appointed you. It's not my place to second guess a client's decision in that regard. I *did* tell her to make sure you would agree to serve because it's quite a time-consuming position, or it can be."

"And what did she say to that?"

He cleared his throat. "You know I can't tell you the substance of my conversations with my client. Clearly, she's gotten around to asking you *post hoc* and you aren't interested in serving. I don't see why you have to make such a production, frankly. All she needs to do is name another—"

"Allison Bennett is dead."

Marsh flinched. "Oh. I'm sorry."

She just looked at him.

He examined the inside of his mug for a moment then he looked up.

"I don't know the nature of your relationship with Ms. Bennett. She did state that you were not a relative. You can always refuse to serve."

She blinked. It was becoming abundantly clear that Marsh had no clue who his client was. Marsh, for all his impeccable manners and good breeding, was just a faceless, interchangeable cog in the Prescott & Talbott machine. He wasn't equipped to deal with the rough edges of his clients' lives.

She took another drink of her fragrant, fresh-roasted coffee while she considered how to break the news to him.

"Hypothetically, what happens if I were to decline the appointment?" she asked in a measured tone.

"That's easy. The probate court appoints someone else to act in your stead. Probably a relative."

"Marsh, the only living relative those kids have is their father."

He shook his head. "I'm afraid you're mistaken. Allison said their father wasn't in the picture. I asked if they were divorced and she said no. Obviously, he predeceased her."

"No, *you're* mistaken. Allison Bennett was living under an assumed name. The father of her six minor children is very much alive. In fact, I'm fairly certain he's the one who killed her."

She'd always thought 'his eyes bulged out' was just an expression, but Marsh's looked like they really were going to pop right out of his head.

"What?!"

"Allison Bennett, formerly known as Anna Bricker, was the estranged wife of Jeffrey Bricker and the star witness for the prosecution at his trial for murder and conspiracy to commit murder. She entered into the witness protection program with her kids, and they all got new identities. But, it appears that Bricker found them."

Marsh's chest heaved.

She leaned back in her chair just in case he was about to vomit.

"Bricker? The escaped felon?"

"That's the one."

"I can't ... Were they divorced?" His cadence changed from blindsided to intrigued almost instantly.

"Pardon?"

"Did Anna Bricker divorce her husband before she became Allison Bennett?"

"I don't know. I doubt it. Everything happened really fast. Why?"

His gray pallor faded, replaced by an excited flush, and he leaned forward.

"Because if she didn't, you just landed smack in the middle of a major case of first impression. This is the stuff of law review articles. Imagine the complexity, Sasha. Did his rights to inherit terminate automatically when she took on a new identity? If not, what effect does Allison Bennett's will have on Anna Bricker's husband? And even beyond the estate issues, this raises novel issues of family law. Does Jeffrey Bricker have any rights to his children? If not, why not."

He actually bounced in his seat, buoyed by the thought of sinking his teeth into such a juicy legal morass.

"I'm glad you find it so interesting, Marsh. As trustee, I gladly accept your offer to represent the children's interests in any litigation arising out of the situation. On a pro bono basis, of course."

The gleam in his eye dimmed slightly. "Pro bono? I'll be glad to handle the case, but I don't think Prescott's going to let me do it for free."

"Make it happen, Marsh. Unless you want to explain to a judge how you failed to satisfy yourself that the documents *you* drafted adequately protected your client's interests."

She drained her coffee and returned the mug to the bar with a *thud.*

"Thanks for the drink," she said over her shoulder as she breezed past him and out of the espresso shop.

15

Cole rubbed his forehead and stared. Cardboard boxes were strewn from one end of the rental house to the other. Bubble wrap and packing peanuts littered the floor, ankle-deep in spots. Butcher paper wound its way along the banister leading to the second floor.

Brianna walked toward him from the back of the house, wading through packing materials. She held a bottle of fancy, organic juice in each hand.

"Want one?" She shoved a strawberry/cherry concoction into his hand.

"Where did this come from?"

"Whole Foods. Calla said she wanted juice. Hank took her to the store and they came back with all sorts of stuff."

"What's all this?" He gestured to the mess.

"Hank said we needed some basics." She shrugged and took a swig of her peach/pineapple/orange smoothie.

He worked his jaw and tried to get a handle on his anger.

"We're not staying here," he finally managed.

She shrugged again. "I guess you should talk to Hank."

"Where is he?"

"Upstairs helping the boys pick out bedrooms."

He pushed the juice back into her hands and ran up the stairs, taking them two at a time, as bubble wrap popped under his feet.

"Be quiet," she called after him. "Leah's putting Calla down for a nap up there."

He skidded to a stop outside one of the four bedrooms on the second floor and peered inside. Hank's big hands gripped one end of a measuring tape. Across the room, Mark held the other end while Hal squatted and peered at the numbers, as if he actually understood what they meant.

Mark looked up and made an 'o' of surprise with his mouth when he saw Cole, breathing heavily, standing in the doorway.

"Oh, hey. We're trying to figure out if the bunk beds will fit in here," he said.

Bunk beds?

"Great. Hey, can I talk to Uncle Hank for a minute?"

Hank must have heard the tightness in his voice. He retracted the measuring tape carefully and handed it to Mark.

"Why don't you guys measure the windows while I talk to your brother?"

He smiled at Hal and strolled casually out into the hallway.

Cole jerked his head toward the bathroom, and Hank followed him into the long, narrow bathroom. It was old but well-kept, with gleaming white subway tiles lining the floor and the walls.

"Something wrong, son?" Hank asked, leaning against the sink.

"Yeah, something's wrong. Why are you setting us up here like we're staying. This is temporary, remember? We can't afford all this stuff just for a couple nights' stay." He tried to control the quaking in his voice but failed.

He actually had no idea what their money situation was. He needed to remember to ask Sasha.

Hank placed a strong hand on his shoulder. "Listen to me now. This *is* just temporary, but while you're here sorting out your mom's estate with Sasha, it's important that you all live as normally as possible. You've been through enough.

Don't go worrying about the cost. It's on Uncle Sam."

Cole exhaled. "Sorry."

Hank patted his arm. "No apologies needed. You're just doing your job as the head of the family, taking care of everyone. I get it. But I'm here to help you, don't forget that."

Cole nodded and blinked back the tears that were building behind his eyes. He didn't trust himself to speak.

After a moment, Hank said, "Come on. You can help us set up the bedrooms."

Cole watched Hank stride out of the bathroom and found himself standing up a little straighter, mimicking the man's confident posture.

16

Sasha huffed in frustration and blew her hair out of her eyes, disturbing Java's nap. The cat squinted at her in displeasure before shifting to a more comfortable position on her lap.

Connelly looked over from the kitchen and caught her eye.

"Everything okay?" he asked, dividing his attention between her and the sourdough he was kneading for bread.

She glanced down at the papers in her hands and tried to frame her answer.

"Not really. Anna Bricker, or Allison Bennett, or whatever you want to call her—she tried to put everything in order, but this is a mess."

She delivered the news matter-of-factly. She

didn't want to panic Connelly, but the reality was what it was. Marsh's ecstatic reaction aside, the situation was not good.

He abandoned his dough, wiped his hands on a dish towel, and walked around the kitchen island. He crouched near Sasha's chair.

"What kind of mess?" he asked.

"The worst kind. Marsh said he called around and located an attorney up near their old house who prepared wills for Jeffrey and Anna Bricker back in 2004. So she has two wills—one in her old name, one in her new name. I don't even ... I have no idea—is the first will invalidated? She left everything to Bricker in the old will. Everything goes into trust for the kids in the new one. She has an old health care power of attorney and an old financial power of attorney, both naming Bricker as her fiduciary agent. Anna Bricker made these documents, but are they binding on Allison Bennett? Well, the health care power of attorney is irrelevant because she's dead now. But that financial power of attorney might have an effect on the irrevocable trust. I mean, maybe not. I don't know. And I *have* to know, don't I? I'm the freaking trustee." She waved the papers at him. "Understand?"

Connelly tilted his head and furrowed his forehead.

"Do I understand? Are you kidding me? No. I have no clue what you're talking about."

She huffed again. This time, Java mewed at her and jumped to the floor. He walked away haughtily.

"Never mind, just take care of your bread. I'll talk to Will and Marsh in the morning. They've been holed up poring over every estate decision published since the eighteen hundreds."

Connelly grabbed her hand. "Talking to Will and that Prescott guy sounds like a good idea. But will you please try to explain just a little bit? I'm worried about those kids."

So was she. The image of Cole's haunted, tired face kept floating across her mind while she wrestled with the myriad potential disasters lurking in the blue-backed estate documents strewn across her lap.

She exhaled. "Okay, sure. I'll walk you through it. Can you finish up that dough and let it rest or whatever it is you do? I could use some fresh air. We can walk and talk."

He rubbed her bare arm. The light pressure sent a shiver along her spine.

"Sure thing. Grab your shoes. I just need a minute."

By unspoken agreement, they headed for Fifth Avenue and Frick Park's gardens—an oasis of green in the concrete city. The smell of jasmine blossoms carried on the warm night air and mixed with exhaust fumes from the buses and cars rumbling past.

Connelly reached for her hand and entwined his fingers through hers. They walked in silence for a moment while she gathered her thoughts.

"Okay, I'm going to try to break this down for you, but I have to warn you, it's complicated."

"What makes it complicated?" he asked. "The fact that the kids are all minors?"

"In part, sure. But the whole thing's a giant, interconnected mess. It's like a final exam essay question dreamed up by the most sadistic law school professor to ever roam the earth ..." she trailed off.

"What?"

"Just thinking of Naya taking all those finals." She shuddered in mock horror.

Connelly rewarded her with a throaty laugh.

"Okay, but seriously, back to the kids."

"Okay. The biggest problem I see is predicting how the law will apply in light of the fact that the Brickers entered WITSEC."

"What difference does WITSEC make?"

"It's the crucial fact—I think. Anna entered into witness protection to prevent Bricker from ever finding her and the kids, right?"

"Yeah, that's the point of the program."

They jogged across Fifth against the light. Connelly nodded to a young couple walking their dog.

After the friendly golden retriever had finished smelling her hand, Sasha continued, "And time was of the essence, right? I mean, pretty much as soon as Anna and the kids stepped foot out of the compound, the government swooped them up and hid them."

"That's more or less true. So?"

"So Anna was issued a new identity right away. She legally changed her name and was assigned a new Social Security Number, correct?"

"Yes. And the same for the kids."

"Right. So, nobody thought to have Anna Bricker initiate divorce proceedings, file for custody, or change her estate plans first."

Connelly stared at her as if she'd suddenly started speaking a foreign language.

"Did they?" she prodded.

"Uh, no. As far as I know, no one did any of those things," he answered in a strained voice.

Sasha exhaled. "Right. So, Anna Bricker and her children no longer exist as far as the government is concerned, but those kids are still alive, Connelly. And Jeffrey Bricker is still their father. I don't see anything in the statute governing the witness protection program that would serve to terminate his right to take under the estate, let alone his parental rights."

"What are you saying? That's crazy, Sasha. They're in the program to protect them from him."

"Actually, that's not completely accurate. They're in the program because their mother was in the program. And that's the other problem. Is there any basis for them to stay in witness protection? None of those kids testified against Bricker. And he hasn't overtly threatened any of them. In fact, assuming he did kill his wife, he can argue that he had the opportunity to kill those kids ... and didn't."

Connelly dropped her hand and stopped in the middle of the path.

"Have you lost your mind? He's a convicted

murderer. An escaped felon on the run. He tried to take us hostage at our wedding. He hunted and slaughtered his wife like an animal."

Sasha placed a gentle hand on his chest to quell the shaking fury that was emanating from him in waves.

"I know all that, honey. But that's not how the law works."

"Of course it is."

"No, it isn't. Estate law is going to apply the documents as they exist unless Marsh and Will can come up with a compelling reason not to. And family law looks to the best interest of the child—" She held up a hand to forestall the objection forming on his lips."— Before you even say it, the fact that Bricker is a demented sociopath isn't determinative. There's Pennsylvania precedent that holds a father who murdered his children's mother is not necessarily an unfit parent. He was deemed not to present a risk to the kids. I'm not saying it's right, I'm saying it's the law."

The anger blazing in Connelly's gray eyes dimmed, replaced by sadness and worry.

"Are you saying Bricker's going to get custody of the Bennett kids?"

"I'm saying I don't know—I can't know, because

I don't know how a court will view the fact that they have new identities."

"This all assumes Bricker will even contest the documents Allison Bennett created, right? Or that he even could. He's on the lam. He can't set foot in a courtroom," Connelly said forcefully.

"I hope that's right. But let's assume that he's eventually recaptured and reincarcerated."

"We don't have to assume that; it's going to happen. It's just a matter of time."

She answered carefully. "Okay, when that happens, he'll be in prison, but he'll be able to try to control me. If I'm the trustee, I'm the only one standing between him and his kids' money. He can toy with me, filing objections to the decisions I make. I'll have no choice but to engage with him."

The words hung on the air between them, heavy.

"We'll make sure that doesn't happen," Connelly insisted even though he had no basis for his certainty.

"Okay, let's leave that aside for the time being. The kids are minors. Who's going to act as their guardian, assuming Bricker is prison? Allison's will doesn't appoint one."

"Why not? Why did she go through all the

trouble of drawing up documents and not name a guardian?"

Sasha considered the question.

"She drew up powers of attorney, too, with no names. Probably because it's a really big decision. She couldn't name a relative—or really anyone she'd known more than a couple months, tops. She probably was hoping to find a friend in North Carolina who she clicked with, develop a relationship, and then amend the documents. I mean, you can't just add six kids to someone's life on a whim."

"True."

"Plus, she probably wasn't sure how WITSEC played into that decision. I mean, if she named a neighbor, would WITSEC have enrolled *that* person into the program—how's that work?"

Connelly searched her face for a long moment.

"I'm not sure what WITSEC would do. When the chief of police came back from his vacation this morning, he called the inspector assigned to Allison Bennett."

"And?"

He coughed into his fist. "And it doesn't sound like they're too happy that the kids were moved up here without anyone consulting them. The inspector and his supervisor are coming up here tomorrow to meet with Hank about it. He asked me to keep an eye on the kids while they're meeting."

"Wait. The rental house, all that furniture—Hank did that all on his own?"

"Yeah."

"What do you think WITSEC will do?"

"I literally have no idea. Protocol would be to move them again, assign them yet another set of new identities. I guess they'll want to act as *de facto* guardian, at least for now."

Her heart sank at the thought of those kids, still reeling from their mother's death, being spirited away yet again.

"They can't do that, Connelly."

The worry in his eyes mirrored her own.

"We'll do what we can to stop it."

"What if we can't?"

From the way he set his jaw, she knew what his response would be before he answered.

"I will."

17

Tuesday night—Wednesday morning

Leo sat on the edge of the bed and watched his wife sleep. Focusing on her gentle, even breathing slowed his pulse, even as his mind continued to race.

I will.

The statement had flown from his mouth before he'd had a chance to consider what it meant, but now it had the weight and ring of a promise. A vow, not unlike the vows he and Sasha had exchanged in front of a moonlit ocean just hours after Bricker's failed attempt to abduct them.

The ache in his chest when he thought of the

six kids who'd lost so much in such a short time convinced him that it was the right decision—even though he had no idea what it entailed.

Sasha hadn't reacted to his vow. She'd just stared at him for a long moment with worry filling her green eyes.

He rose to his feet and crept soundlessly across the exposed wood floor. He pressed his forehead against the cool window pane and searched the dark night. He didn't know what he was looking for. Bricker hiding in the shrubbery?

He shook his head to rid it of the ridiculous image and turned toward the stairs. If he couldn't sleep, he might as well do something productive. He padded down the stairs to the kitchen, dodging the cat, who darted from the bed, hoping to score a midnight snack.

He sprinkled some treats on the counter for Java and poured himself a glass of water. While he waited for his laptop to complete its startup routine, he sipped the water and scrolled through his new emails on his phone. Nothing urgent.

He snagged his key chain from the small drawer near the sink and activated the wireless security fob. When the small white light blinked, he rolled his index finger across the sensor window and waited for the biometric program to recognize his fingerprint and provide a one-time password. As the digits and letters scrolled across the thumbnail-sized screen he copied them into the password field on his laptop screen.

A cheerful blip informed him that he was in.

He returned the key chain to its spot for safekeeping. Hank encouraged him to simply attach his house and car keys to the thing and carry it around but Leo regarded the device with equal parts awe and suspicion, so back in the drawer it went.

He navigated to the link Hank had set up for the Allison Bennett matter and scrolled through the files in the folder. As Hank received official reports from the local police and from within the various federal agencies working the matter, he placed copies in the folder. Leo was certain Hank wasn't authorized to share the documents, but Hank operated in a world where authorization was honored in the breach.

He scanned the files, looking for the most recent documents. The Department of Justice had drafted a memo in advance of WITSEC's meeting with Hank.

He grinned. Leave it to the government to be so compartmentalized and feudal that Hank had been able to get someone to fork over a copy of the secret memo prepared to lay out WITSEC's strategy for a meeting with him.

He double-clicked on the PDF. His grin morphed into a soft groan when the document opened. Apparently, Justice was paying its lawyers by the word. Eighty-six single-spaced pages? Some junior lawyer hadn't slept since the murder.

He snuck a longing gaze at the coffee maker, but decided against brewing a pot. As much as he'd like to tackle the memo with a steaming mug of caffeine in hand, he knew Sasha too well: as soon as the smell of fresh coffee wafted upstairs, she'd be awake and out of bed. She needed to sleep. He'd make do with water.

The dense memo was marked "Not for External Distribution." Despite its wordiness, it was a riveting read. The author began with an executive summary of the issues raised by Allison Bennett's death, the history of WITSEC, and a recommended course of action. The next section laid out the same points in greater detail, with support from federal legislation and legislative history and some federal case law, which the drafter took pains to note was not directly on point.

The memo focused on the central question that Sasha had raised during their walk to the park: what were the government's rights and responsibilities with regard to the Bennett children in light of the murder of their mother?

It laid out the possible scenarios and determined that the Marshal's Service probably had no legal right to keep the children in the witness protection program. The memo went on to advise that if the children wished to stay in the program, the Justice Department should take the position that they could do so. The author acknowledged—in a footnote set out in font so tiny that Leo had to squint to read it—that the Bennett children were not entitled by statute to remain in the program once the protected witness (their mother) had exited it, either voluntarily or otherwise, but urged that, in light of the situation, the government owed the motherless children a moral duty, if not a legal one.

And, apparently, not unaware that counseling his employer to do the right thing was a losing argument, the author cited the possibility of a public relations disaster and politically motivated scandal if the public learned that the kids had been unceremoniously dumped after the government had failed to live up to its promise to protect their mother.

The final assessment was that the Marshal's Service should offer to immediately relocate the

Bennett children into foster care, perhaps with families already participating in the program. If they declined and chose to leave the program, then the U.S. government could take the position that it had done all it could to assist them.

He sat back and blinked at the screen as if that would change the words. WITSEC's plan was to offer to split up the kids and farm them out to mafioso informers and drug dealers scattered across the country, knowing full well the offer would be rejected.

He was so stunned that he didn't hear Sasha descending the steps.

"What are you doing up?" she asked from the kitchen.

He jumped, startled by her voice, and hurried to close Adobe.

"Geez, you scared me. I couldn't sleep. You?"

He glanced at the laptop screen, which now displayed the list of files within the Bennett folder. He casually eased the lid shut. He was surprised to see how much time had passed. It was nearly five a.m.

She noted his sneakiness with a knowing look but didn't comment on it.

"Java leapt onto my face. Kind of hard to sleep through that sort of battery."

She smiled sleepily and flipped the switch to turn on the coffee maker then crossed the room to join him in the living room. She arched her back from side to side then stretched her arms over her head, one then the other.

He gave her his full attention for his favorite part of her morning stretching routine—the deep back bend she pulled off as if it were effortless.

She brought herself back to upright in one fluid motion.

"What?" she asked.

"What what?"

"You're staring at me."

He let a lazy smile play across his face. "Just enjoying the view."

"Uh, oh."

He loved that he could still fluster his wife.

"Anyway, what are you working on?" she asked.

He stood up and tilted her chin up to meet his gaze.

"You wouldn't be changing the subject, now, would you, Counselor?" he asked.

She grinned and fluttered her eyelashes. "You wouldn't be trying to distract me, now, would you, Agent Connelly?"

He burst out laughing, louder than their banter

warranted, but it felt good to laugh after all the worry and tension of the past few days.

"Guilty as charged."

She shook her head and clucked her tongue in mock disapproval.

"Why don't I pour us some coffee and meet you back in bed to confer about this matter in more detail?"

"I think that's a good plan. Why don't we skip the coffee?" he suggested as he strode up the stairs.

"Bite your tongue," she ordered as she pulled two mugs down from the cabinet.

"I'd rather not. I have other plans for it," he tossed over his shoulder.

Peals of laughter erupted from within the kitchen.

18

Wednesday

Bricker flexed his hands to keep them loose and shook his legs to ease the cramping. The McCandless woman worked long hours, and he wasn't as young as he used to be. He dearly hoped she had a court appointment or a workout scheduled so he could move around some.

He settled back on his bench and considered his options once more.

He didn't have time to watch her for weeks on end to learn her patterns and routines. Waiting for her to let her guard down was also a useless plan—

she was too alert to wander around inattentively. And, more often than not, she traveled with her husband glued to her side.

He was either going to have to get lucky or find someone to help him.

Bricker was of the view that relying on luck was a loser's plan, so he resolved to reach out to the Westmoreland County preppers who'd transported him from Bridgeville to Pittsburgh.

He settled back against the rusting dumpster behind her office building and trained his eyes on the pair of windows that he knew were hers. He wished, not for the first time, that he had been able to get his hands on a decent pair of binoculars in his travels. He missed his military-grade Steiners.

McCandless flitted by the window, her long hair streaming behind her, in an evident hurry. Two other figures—male, otherwise nondescript, followed her.

He leaned forward in anticipation. Maybe something was finally going to happen.

He risked exposure to adjust his position so that he could see both the rear door and the main entrance to the building.

He heard the metal door scraping open and pressed himself against the building's side wall.

He caught the middle of a conversation as

McCandless, Volmer, and a stranger stepped out onto the gravel parking lot.

"...unusual for a probate court to grant a hearing this quickly, even on an emergency petition."

Volmer nodded, serious and focused, at what the stranger was saying.

The new man had to be another lawyer. He could have passed for Volmer's brother, Bricker thought as he crept along the wall and tracked the trio to the Passat he recognized as McCandless' vehicle.

He strained to get a better look. Two tall, thin men. Late middle-aged. Well-made suits. Conservative ties. Expensive trial bags. Steel-rimmed glasses. Forget brothers; they could have been twins.

McCandless walked between them. She was a good foot shorter than both men, but as usual she kept her head on a swivel. Left, right, repeat. She set the brisk pace.

The other two walked along obliviously.

Soft targets.

But, unfortunately, he needed to hit her, not them.

"Why do you think the judge set the hearing so fast? It's not as though he had time to have a law clerk research all the issues you raised. And they're clearly issues of first impression," Volmer asked.

The other man shrugged while McCandless activated her car's keyless entry feature.

"Judge Kumpar is a solid jurist. I'm sure he recognizes the need to act quickly to sort out the effect of the witness protection program on the disposition of the Bennett estate."

The three lawyers slid into the car while Bricker tried to stay steady on his feet.

Witness protection program? The Bennett estate?

His face grew hot, and his vision swam.

Was that little witch representing Anna's estate?

His surprise was short-lived, the shock turning to renewed fury.

He had to get to the courthouse and figure out a way to learn what happened during this hearing. It would be far too great a risk for him to walk into the courtroom, so he'd need to find an ally. Unfortunately, Pittsburgh's urban prepper movement was heavy on attention-hungry dilettantes but light on true believers. His months on the run had taught him that the next best thing to a real survivalist was a homeless man of certain age and bearing—usually a Vietnam vet.

As McCandless eased the car along the uneven lot, he shrank back between the buildings and fumbled for his wallet. He'd spent the night at the city bus depot, thanks to a friend of the movement. He'd liberated a fistful of bus passes and committed the city bus routes to memory before he left. At the time, he'd had the idle thought that if a man wanted to drive home the point that government was a sham, nothing but a mirage, wreaking havoc on a municipality's public transportation system was an effective way to do so. Once he had taken care of his personal business, perhaps he could return to spreading the movement's message.

McCandless & Volmer's law offices were located just above the EBO, or East Busway, a dedicated express track for trips from the city's East End to Downtown. He ran along a short alley, hopped a low wall, and vaulted down the cement steps to the busway below. A handful of late commuters milled at the stop with their heads bent over their various smartphones. The only traveler not distracted by her Facebook feed or the latest headlines and not on a quest to bust bubbles, gather gems, or otherwise anesthetize herself from the world had her hands full with two small children in a double stroller.

Bricker had been railing against the mass adoption of technological opiates for more than a decade, but, at this moment, he was profoundly grateful for their addictive nature. None of these people would notice him, let alone be able to describe him. And the mother, with what appeared to be a jelly handprint on her blouse, was too busy trying to keep the curly-haired girl from climbing out of the stroller while simultaneously replacing the soft-soled shoes her twin brother delighted in kicking off his feet.

He was invisible.

A silver bus pulled up alongside the concrete shelter, and the driver opened the doors with a *whoosh* of compressed air. As the waiting group stowed their devices in pockets, purses, and bags, Bricker sidestepped the woman struggling with the stroller and flashed the one-zone pass at the driver.

He chose a seat in the middle of the bus and turned to stare out the window at the cement jungle surrounding him.

19

Judge Kumpar ran his courtroom like a CEO. His efficiency and directness were a marked contrast to the usual milling around, throat-clearing, and disarray that Sasha had always considered the hallmarks of the Allegheny Court of Common Pleas.

Maybe things were different in probate court, but she had been unable to hide her surprise when the clerk who checked them in had the entire docket and seemed to expect them—no missing documents, no confused questions about why they were there.

Will, who spent as little time in state court as she did, seemed to be equally taken aback by the difference between the Orphan's Court Division and the rest of the system.

Only Marsh was unfazed. Well, as unfazed as Marshall Alverson, professional worrier, could possibly be. As if to undercut any confidence she might have in him, he reached down and hiked up his trousers with his free hand.

To her endless amusement, he was actually wearing both a belt and suspenders. She could only assume he had recurring nightmares about losing his pants in court.

In addition to his sartorial challenges, Marsh was so nervous he was shaking. Like most attorneys who specialize in estate work, he rarely saw the inside of a courtroom. Will had promised him he wouldn't have to handle the argument, he just needed to serve as their guide. He was performing that duty beautifully—he knew the procedures and protocols cold. He also knew the facts and the issues cold. But he was out of his element, and she and Will had to respect that. She sure wouldn't want to be thrown into a public offering drafting session or a labor negotiation.

She gave Marsh a reassuring smile.

The clerk nodded toward the door leading from Judge Kumpar's chambers as if to indicate it was show time. A moment later, right on time, the door swung open and the judge strode toward the bench.

While the clerk announced that court was session, Sasha studied the judge's tanned, unlined face. He had small, bright eyes and a quick smile. A gray streak ran through his dark hair. Instead of the aloof, dignified demeanor so common among judges on the federal bench, Judge Kumpar gave off a brisk, 'let's get down to business' vibe.

He nodded to his clerk and then turned to the assembled lawyers.

"Counselors, good morning."

"Good morning, Your Honor," Sasha replied.

"Your Honor," Will echoed.

They all looked at Marsh, who was studying a copy of the motion.

Sasha jabbed him with her elbow.

He looked up, startled, and pushed his glasses up on the bridge of his nose.

"Uh, apologies. Good morning, Judge."

"Mr. Alverson. It's nice to see you." The judge leaned forward and nodded at Sasha and Will. "And your colleagues. Welcome to Orphans' Court. You'll see that probate isn't quite as adversarial as trial court, and I don't stand on formality. So let's do this, as the kids say."

"Yes, sir."

"Very good, Your Honor," Will said. Sasha

hoped he wasn't trying to match the judge's informality; if so, he was failing.

The judge lifted the top sheet from the tidy stack in front of him.

"Ms. McCandless, you've been named trustee of an irrevocable testamentary trust for the benefit of the minor Bennett children."

"Yes, Your Honor."

"That's a problem, wouldn't you say?"

It *was* a problem, it was a huge, hairy problem for approximately a half a million reasons. But she wasn't sure which problem the judge had zeroed in on.

"It could be," she allowed.

The judge pushed his glasses up on to the top of his head and rested them in his hair, like a high school girl at the beach.

"Well, let's see. The decedent, Allison Bennett, formerly known as Anna Bricker, married one Jeffrey Bricker and bore a half dozen children to him, right?"

"Right."

"Mr. Bricker may have many flaws—and judging from Mr. Alverson's brief, not to mention news reports, some of them are real doozies—but lifelessness doesn't appear to be one of them. That is, the children have a father. Who is living. And who, it appears, takes under an earlier will. Unless you know something I don't know about his vital statistics."

Will cleared his throat. "We'd argue that Anna Bricker repudiated that will, even before she executed the new one. The day she changed her identity and entered the witness protection program she left behind her former life and all its vestiges."

"Poetic. Any support for that in case law, counselor?"

"Um, no."

The judge opened his mouth to respond but stopped when the door to the courtroom swung inward.

A disheveled, dirty man shuffled into the room. He smiled sheepishly and took a seat in the back row of the otherwise empty gallery.

The judge clamped his mouth shut for a moment. He tapped his index finger on the stack of papers, thinking.

Sasha wondered what he'd do. The courts were open to the public. It was a cornerstone of the system. Even if Judge Kumpar suspected the man was simply looking for a cool place to rest, he couldn't very well kick him out. But they'd have to dance around the issue of the Bennett children's identities. It would make drilling down into the issues that much harder—not to mention less efficient.

Will shifted and looked at the man over his shoulder. Sasha followed his gaze. He blinked back at them, guileless but nervous.

The judge clapped his hands together, once, to get everyone's attention.

Sasha had seen preschool teachers use the tactic, but never a judge.

"Given the issues of first impression raised by this case, it's not appropriate for the probate court to act without first addressing the issue of the father's standing."

"Standing to take under the will, Your Honor?" Marsh stammered.

"No. I'm afraid we need to begin somewhere much more fundamental: we need to address his parental rights."

Judge Kumpar spread his hands apart in a gesture that said 'what else can I do?'

"I've already consulted with Judge Perry-Brown, and she's ready for you," the judge explained.

"Pardon?" Will asked in a strangled voice.

"We've sort of divvied up the Orphan's Court responsibilities informally. I handle the probate matters, and she handles termination of parental rights and adoptions. Cass Myers does the incapacitation hearings. Carving up the cases into little areas of expertise works well for us. Unfortunately for you, though, that means I have to kick you over to Judge Perry-Brown to determine whether the father's parental rights should be terminated."

"Of course, Your Honor," Sasha murmured.

To her right, Will was nodding along in disappointed agreement. To her left, Marsh was doing a terrible job of hiding his excited relief. Once they got kicked to Judge Perry-Brown, he could go back to his tastefully appointed office and surround himself with codicils and affidavits.

"But you're in luck. Judge Perry-Brown just moved to a new courtroom and has reserved this morning to deal with setting up her new chambers. So there's nothing on her schedule, and she's agreed to see you now." Judge Kumpar beamed.

"Thank you, Your Honor," Sasha said, smiling back at him. It wasn't as though he was going to change his mind, so there was no point in pouting.

"One final question, though, Ms. McCandless. Just so I'm clear when this matter returns to probate, will you agree to serve as the trustee?"

She felt Will and Marsh turn their eyes to her. Marsh had explained repeatedly, in painful detail, that she could decline the appointment.

Serving as trustee would entail years of monthly visits with Judge Kumpar to update the court on the status of the trust and to answer any questions he might have. It would also entail filing sheaves of financial reports to account for the funds in the trust.

She certainly didn't need *more* paperwork and *more* appointments in her life.

But Allison had chosen her for a reason.

And the kids needed *someone*.

The room was silent. Everyone was waiting.

"I will, Your Honor."

The words felt almost as weighty as her wedding vows.

"Super!" He clapped his hands together again, this time with something approaching glee. Then he gathered up his papers and stood.

Before his clerk could get out the words to dismiss court, the judge was gone in a blur of robes.

"Judge Perry-Brown is in Courtroom 6," the clerk said.

"Thank you," Marsh answered.

He turned to Sasha and Will. "Well, I'll leave this in your capable hands. Once Judge Perry-Brown's ruled, reach out to me, and we'll keep the probate ball rolling."

"I will. Thanks for your help, Marsh," Sasha said.

"Yes. And give our best to everyone back at the office," Will added, ever the diplomat.

Marsh nodded and scurried off.

"Well, this should be fun," Will remarked, as they gathered up their papers. "I don't suppose you know anything about Judge Perry-Brown?"

"Never heard of her," Sasha confirmed.

They walked in silence out of the courtroom.

JUDGE PERRY-BROWN'S courtroom was unlocked when they arrived. A cluster of people filled the back row of her gallery.

"I never realized the state court buffs were such back-benchers," Sasha whispered to Will as they hurried to the counsel table.

It was sort of odd how they sat in the back, considering they were there voluntarily. In law school, the back-benchers tended to occupy the rear row of the class because they were

unprepared, unengaged, or otherwise unhappy to be in class. At least, that was her impression, as a dyed-in-the-wool, front row gunner.

Will craned his neck to eyeball the senior citizens with their heads bent over their Sudoku puzzles.

"Isn't that the guy from Kumpar's courtroom?" he whispered back, jerking his head toward a man on the far end.

Sasha peered at him. He was rumpled and rough-looking but other than that, she couldn't say. He had his head bowed.

"Maybe?"

They dropped their bags on the table and walked up to the front desk to check in with Judge Perry-Brown's courtroom clerk.

"Hi," Sasha said, sliding a business card onto the desk. "Sasha McCandless and Will Volmer. Judge Kumpar sent us over?"

The clerk examined the card for a moment, rhythmically clicking the top of her ballpoint pen as she did so.

"Your firm info the same as hers?" the woman asked Will.

"Yes."

She scribbled his name under Sasha's printed title and clipped the card to a file.

"Okay. Have a seat. Judge'll be out in a minute. We're just waiting for Old Big Gun." She smirked.

Will cocked his head and gave the woman a puzzled look.

Sasha's heart thumped.

"Excuse me? Big Gun? Do you mean Andy Pulaski?" she asked.

"You know another one?"

"Um, I'm not sure I follow. Why are we waiting for Mr. Pulaski?" Will asked.

"Your guess is as good as mine. Judge said call him and tell him to get his butt over here, so I did. I imagine we'll all find out when he shows up."

Sasha swallowed around the lump in her throat and hurried back to the table.

"Are you okay?" Will asked her in a low voice as he slid into the seat next to her.

She pasted on a smile to ease his worry.

"I'm fine."

Will's eyes narrowed as if he didn't believe her.

His skepticism was understandable. He was almost as well-acquainted with the hard-charging, ethically-challenged divorce attorney who called himself Big Gun as she was.

The psychic scars from her tangles with Andy Pulaski had finally healed. She couldn't believe he was popping his head up again like a rat or a groundhog or ... well, whatever kind of rodent lived underground and popped its head up. She was a city girl, after all.

"What the devil do you think Pulaski has to do

with any of this?" Will mused, more to himself than to her.

She shrugged. The last time she crossed paths with Pulaski she'd been representing two men accused of murdering their estranged wives, both of whom had been partners at Sasha and Will's former firm. Pulaski was the divorce attorney who represented both of the women. And, as it turned out, the man who killed Ellen Laing worked for him as a messenger. That would have been enough to put a bad taste in anyone's mouth, but it was only half the story.

Pulaski's messenger had also been convicted of killing Clarissa—wrongly, as it turned out. The right man was in prison now, but that mistake had weighed on Sasha for a long time. It had nearly cost her her relationship with Connelly, her mental health, and her life.

Suffice it to say if she ever saw Andy Pulaski again, it would be too soon.

And then, like a set piece in a bad sitcom, there he was. Huffing, out of breath, and racing up the aisle to the counsel table.

Pulaski dropped a battered briefcase on the table, smoothed his hair, running a hand over his low ponytail, and straightened his garish purple tie. His eyes widened with recognition at the sight of Sasha, but he clicked his game face into place almost instantly.

"Counselors," he said by way of greeting as he struggled to catch his breath.

"Andy," Will responded.

Sasha just nodded.

"What's this all about?" Pulaski asked Will.

"I suppose we'll all find out together. Even the judge's clerk doesn't know why you're here."

Pulaski made a clicking noise with his tongue and flopped into the vacant chair next to Sasha.

For reasons she had never fully understood, some state courtrooms provided a single table for all counsel and parties to share, rather than the more common set up of having defendants and plaintiffs sit at separate tables. It made for a crowded, uncomfortable situation—particularly for the two opponents sitting closest to each other. Surely the legislature could find room in its budget to order some additional tables?

She scooted her chair closer to Will's and resisted the urge to ask him to switch seats with her. This wasn't seventh grade, she reminded herself.

Either oblivious to or unfazed by her discomfort, Pulaski leaned over and stage whispered, "How've you been? Heard you got hitched. Good for you. If it doesn't work out, have your husband give me a call."

He fake laughed, a hearty guffaw.

Will turned and gave him a withering gaze.

Sasha stared straight ahead for a long moment then looked at him as if he hadn't spoken and remarked, "Why don't you go check in with the clerk so we can get on with this?"

He remained seated, waved his arm, and shouted toward the front of the room, "Hey, Bev, I'm here!"

"I noticed, Andy. The judge will be out in a minute."

The clerk returned to her paperwork with an expression that looked as though she smelled something putrid.

So that was how it was going to be. Pulaski had a reputation as an unpleasant, combative jerk to uphold. The only way to react was to refuse to react.

Sasha smiled to herself. That sounded like something her favorite Buddhist would say.

"Something funny?" Pulaski asked.

She was saved from having to answer by the appearance of the judge.

"All rise. The Honorable Merry Perry-Brown presiding," Bev the clerk intoned.

Merry Perry? The judge's parents must have had a sense of humor, Sasha thought. She stifled a giggle and felt Pulaski giving her the side-eye.

"Good morning," the judge said, smiling broadly to show off a dazzling smile that seemed out of place with her frizzy hair and wrinkled robe.

"Good morning, Your Honor," Sasha and Will sing-songed before returning their seats.

Pulaski went on the attack immediately.

"With all respect, Your Honor, can I know what this is about? I have a full day of meetings and conferences, but my secretary received a call from your chambers demanding that I drop everything and—"

The judge raised her hand and cut him off. "Enough." She turned to Sasha and Will. "Ms. McCandless and Mr. Volmer, I take it?"

They popped back to their feet.

"Yes, Your Honor."

"Welcome. And where is Mr. Alverson? Will he be joining us?" she asked.

"No, Your Honor. Mr. Volmer and I thought his presence wasn't necessary at this time."

"Very good. In that case, we'll get started. To answer your question, Mr. Pulaski, the court has decided to appoint you to represent the father in Ms. McCandless and Mr. Volmer's matter."

Pulaski sputtered. "A court appointment? I don't have time to take on another case, judge."

The judge's megawatt smile vanished. "I'll be blunt, Mr. Pulaski. You have clogged the docket, not only of this court, but of every judge in the Family Division, with your endless motions and briefs, which range from the frivolous to the laughable to the downright nasty. Well, I have a client who is the perfect match for you. In fact, I can't think of another member of the bar better suited to represent Mr. Bricker than Big Gun Pulaski."

Pulaski frowned and scanned the room. "Bricker? That name sounds familiar. Well, where is he? I guess we need to confer."

"Mr. Bricker is currently a fugitive, Mr. Pulaski. Having escaped from a federal prison, he's understandably keeping a low profile. He is, nonetheless, entitled to representation in a proceeding to terminate his parental rights. Accordingly, you will represent him."

Pulaski was shaking his head. "No way. Not that Bricker."

"Yes, that Bricker. And yes, Mr. Pulaski, you will represent him." The judge leaned forward and softened her tone. "Andrew, I've known you for a long time. You've created a persona that has made it difficult for litigants, lawyers, and the court. Now it's time to pay the piper. Ms. McCandless has a will to probate. There are six children who need to get on with their lives. We aren't all going to be held hostage by some escaped convict."

"Will? Who's dead? I have no idea what's going on here. Someone's going to have to fill me in." Pulaski's head swiveled from the judge to Sasha and Will then back to the judge.

Judge Perry-Brown puckered her mouth and surveyed the row of onlookers.

"Ladies and gentlemen, sorry to disappoint you all but I don't have anything on the calendar this morning. Judge Clark next door usually puts on a good show, though."

As the audience packed up their newspapers and tablets and started filing out of the courtroom, she turned back to the assembled lawyers.

"Given the sensitive nature of the matter, we'll do this in chambers. You'll have to pardon the disarray; I'm in the middle of moving."

She left the bench and headed for the door to her private chambers. The clerk held it open and waited while Sasha, Will, and Pulaski gathered their belongings and followed suit.

20

A shadow fell across the flattened cardboard box where Bricker sat, his legs outstretched and back against the cool brick wall, in the same pose as the other denizens of the alley that ran behind the courthouse.

He looked up.

The man—he'd given his name as Pat Brown, and Bricker neither knew nor cared if that were his real name—grinned down at him.

"Thanks for saving my spot, friend."

"Don't mention it." Bricker stood and dusted off the seat of his khakis. "Well?"

Pat rolled his eyes skyward and thought for a moment.

"Okay, the judge was already talking when I got

there, so I missed the first part but he said that he, uh, couldn't do anything with the will until Mr. Bricker's rights were worked out."

"You're sure? He said Bricker?"

"Yeah, man. The second judge did, too."

"Second judge?"

"I was getting to that. He said he was sending the lawyers over to this lady judge right away. I figured I should go, too. That was cool, right?"

Pat looked worried, as if he might not get the promised twenty dollars because he'd used his independent judgment.

"Yes, you did the right thing. Good thinking," Bricker reassured him.

He hoped Pat hadn't drawn too much attention to himself, but ultimately he was disposable if necessary.

The homeless man beamed at him. "Okay, good. So I went over to the other courtroom and there were already a bunch of geezers sitting there, so I sat with them. Two of the lawyers from the will judge's courtroom came over—the little woman and one of the dudes. I don't know where the other guy went."

Bricker did.

He'd seen the stranger from McCandless' office taking the wide courthouse steps two at a time about a half an hour earlier. The man had crossed the alley and continued along Grant Street into a glass office tower.

"Don't worry about him. What happened with the second judge?"

Pat scratched his right ear.

"Well they sat around for a bit waiting for this other lawyer to show up. Man, that guy was a piece of work. Name of, uh, Pulaski, Pulkowski, Pilarski—some Polish something or other. Anyhow, he must act like a real tough guy in court. The other two lawyers treated him like he stunk or something. Especially the chick. She wanted nothing to do with him. And the judge lit into him. She more or less said since he was such a scuzzball, she was appointing him to represent some scumbag client."

"Oh?"

"Yeah. The Bricker guy broke out of prison and is on the run, but she needs to make a decision about terminating his rights before they can probate that will you're interested in."

Pat's eyes narrowed. Bricker could see the wheels turning. Time to wrap it up before Pat got too curious for his own good.

"Hmm. So was that it?"

"Judge decided to do the rest back in her office. So I left. I got a friend, though. One of the guys who runs the security scanner sometimes brings me breakfast. I could find out when there's another hearing and maybe do the same thing again?"

Bricker had to give him credit for his eagerness to work.

"Maybe. I'll let you know. If I need to find you again, will you be here?"

Pat nodded. "Rain or shine. Been kicked out of most of the shelters in town because I like a nip now and then."

Bricker peeled off a twenty from the roll of bills stowed in his left pants pocket. Then he added another couple of twenties and pressed them into Pat's filthy hand.

"Here you go. Twenty for your services, as agreed. Take the rest to the Army Surplus Store and get yourself a decent sleeping bag. Or a parka. Don't drink it."

He turned on his heel and walked out of the narrow space before the man could react to his charity.

21

Sasha was putting together a medieval-themed Lego set with Leah and Mark at the kitchen table when she heard Connelly's footsteps in the hall. She glanced up. His cheek muscle twitched, even as he smoothed his expression into a smile for the kids.

Tense, she thought. The meeting with WITSEC must not have gone well.

Connelly had been waiting in her office when she returned from her morning spent bouncing around state court. After expressing appropriate horror at the news that Andy Pulaski had been appointed to represent Bricker, he said he needed a small favor.

The small favor had turned out to be babysitting all the kids while he and Hank met with WITSEC.

She caught Connelly's eye and raised a brow.

He nodded, almost imperceptibly, then said, "What are you guys working on?"

"Some castle. It has eleventy-million parts." She was only slightly exaggerating.

Mark snorted. "It's easy. It just takes patience."

Leah slid out of her chair. "If it's so easy, you can finish it by yourself. Leo and Sasha can help me figure out the garden since Brianna won't."

"What won't Brianna do?" Sasha asked.

The girl stuck out her lower lip. "She's the one who got Mom's green thumb, but she won't help me plot out a garden. We need to have a garden." Her voice cracked and went up an octave.

Mark dropped the turret pieces and hurried to the other side of the table to put an arm around his sister.

Connelly feinted forward as if he were going to try to help comfort the girl. Sasha shook her head and gestured toward the doorway.

As Mark shushed his sobbing sister, Connelly followed Sasha into the hallway.

"We should do something to take her mind off it," he whispered.

"No. They've suffered a loss. They need to

mourn. And, trust me, she'd rather be with her brother now than some random adults."

He twisted his mouth into a skeptical knot, but she pressed on.

"Trust me, Connelly. You're an only child—you don't understand. Mark can help her better than we can. They have a bond."

As she said the words, she realized she was thinking of her own brothers and the way they'd all come together when Patrick, the oldest, was killed.

She cleared her throat and pushed the thought out of her mind. *Not now.*

Connelly furrowed his brow and stared hard at her.

"Thinking about Patrick?" he asked in a low, gentle voice.

She blinked. "How do you do that?"

He pulled her close. "I know my wife."

She allowed herself a moment to rest her head against his warm chest and listen to the steady rhythm of his heart. Then she leaned back to tilt her head up and meet his eyes.

"You do. And I know my husband. What happened with Hank?"

His jaw tightened for a brief moment. Then he exhaled. "He wants to update you and Will tomorrow. Right now, he's off on some sort of top-secret day trip, but let's just say WITSEC is looking to wash its hands of the Bennett kids."

"Wash its hands how?"

His cheek twitched. "Hank was told that if he insisted on continuing to have contact with the kids, they were out of the program effective immediately."

She felt her mouth drop open and clamped it shut.

"On what grounds?"

"He's a person from their past. That's against the rules. If he agreed to cut off all ties with the Bennetts and you agreed to decline to serve as trustee, then they would immediately swoop in and relocate the kids again. They'd get new identities, and we'd never see them again."

"What did Hank say?"

His lips quirked into a smile. "It involved the inspector's mother and a barnyard animal. I don't think you want me to repeat it."

She giggled but got serious again right away. "What about Bricker's parental rights issue? They would just move the kids again and hide them from their admittedly insane and criminal father? Don't they think that needs to be resolved?"

"Come on, Sasha. This is your post-September

11 government we're talking about. Security trumps all."

"Seriously? That's *my* line. And need I remind you, you *are* them."

He shook his head. "No. Hank and I, we don't let politics—national, office, or otherwise—cloud our judgment. You have to know that." He grabbed her shoulders. "It's important that you understand that."

"Connelly, jeez, I was just giving you a hard time."

"Sorry. I'm just a little on edge. First you tell me that dirtball Pulaski is representing Bricker, then we have that meeting."

"It's going to be okay. So what's the plan for the kids while Hank's not around?"

He cleared his throat. "Actually, Hank asked me if we'd consider staying here with them until their situation gets straightened out."

"Stay here? What did you say?"

"I said I had to talk to you, of course. But you should know he's going crazy playing babysitter."

She could believe it. Hank was a confirmed bachelor. Former military. A man of routines.

Having grown up in a big family, one thing she knew was that routines flew straight out the window when balancing the needs of multiple kids came into the picture. Even Valentina, her fastidious mother, had thrown up her hands and gone with the flow on more occasions than not. Hank was hardly a go-with-the-flow kind of guy.

"Live here?"

"Temporarily."

She considered fussing, but she knew she'd say yes in the end. And she had some things to take care of.

"Okay. We're going to need to get food. I fed this crew lunch, but the refrigerator is pretty empty."

He shrugged. "Why don't you run out and get some stuff then we can ask Naya to come over and hang out while we go back to the condo, grab Java, and pack up some stuff?"

Her brain was stuck on the first part of his suggestion.

"What makes you think I know how to grocery shop for six kids any better than you do? My uterus didn't come with instructions, you know."

He swallowed a laugh as Mark poked his head out into the hall.

"Uh, hey."

"Hey. How's your sister?" she asked.

"Sad, but better. Can one of you help her out? She grabbed some of my mom's seeds before we left, and she really wants to plant them. Like a memorial or something." He stared down at his feet.

"Sure. I will. Sasha's on her way out to the store." Connelly tossed her the car keys.

She snagged the keys and gave Connelly a mock glare.

At least she knew how to grocery shop. She didn't know the first thing about gardening.

"I'll be back in a bit. But I need to run an errand first."

He cocked his head. "What kind of errand?"

"I'm going to stop by and see Daniel. I want to borrow something from him."

22

Daniel re-sheathed the fixed-blade knife and weighed the weapon in his right palm for a moment before passing it to Sasha. She took it in her left hand and turned the sheath to the side then slid it out to examine the blade more closely.

"Thanks again," she said.

Daniel waved off her gratitude with an impatient gesture.

"Don't mention it. I mean that literally. If Chris or my father—or God forbid, your father—finds out I gave you a knife ... I don't even want to think about it."

"I'm not going to tell anyone. In any case, it's not as if I'm not perfectly capable of wreaking havoc without a weapon." She shot him a look.

He matched her look with an irritated glare.

"Right. But now you're armed. Armed. Think about that for a minute. It's antithetical to everything Krav Maga teaches, not to mention everything you believe. Your brother was killed—"

"Don't." She held up her empty hand, palm forward, in a motion that said 'stop.' "Please don't. Just walk me through using this, okay?" She was surprised to hear that her voice sounded forceful and even. She was shaking like a wet dog inside.

He sighed heavily.

"Okay. First of all, it's not a training knife. It's a real combat blade, so bear that in mind."

Unlike the traditional martial arts, Krav Maga instruction didn't include any ritualized weapons forms. No hamkudo, the Korean sword discipline; no staff fighting; no nunchuck training, so common in karate.

Instead Krav Maga emphasized street fighting and self-defense. The best weapon a Krav Maga practitioner could employ was her legs, to walk (or run) away from a brewing conflict. Second best was her voice, to diffuse the situation. A distant third was her hands, only when contact was unavoidable.

The philosophy was ingrained in both teacher and student.

But given Sasha's recent past, they'd also agreed that some training in warding off knife and gun attacks was warranted—a not unreasonable position considering she'd been the target of both attacks more than once. That said, their training focus had been on responding to a weapons assault while unarmed.

After all, as a civil litigator, non-hunter, and urban dweller, Sasha was usually unarmed. Unless one counted the deadly geisha hairpin she occasionally used to twist her hair up into a knot.

This, however, was not a typical situation. She was helping to care for six children whose father may or may not be stalking them. It was beyond dispute that he was stalking her. She wanted a weapon. Not a gun, not with all those kids in the house—and not with the baggage of her brother's death hanging over her. But a knife. A knife with a sharp, wicked blade.

"I'll be careful."

Daniel accepted her promise with a small nod. "You sure you're going to be okay with this?"

She followed his gaze. He was staring at her left bicep. The arm that Wally Stewart had slashed a year earlier, severing her carotid artery and nearly killing her. The scar was faint, nothing more than a thin, white whisper against her freckled skin. But Daniel knew. He'd seen how the wound had weakened her dominant side. He'd helped her rebuild her power over several long months.

Of course he'd be worried about her getting into a knife fight. Krav Maga worked by teaching students to react instinctively in a combat situation, not stopping and thinking. Would she be able to turn off her emotional reaction in the event of another knife attack or would her brain slow her down?

"I'm not going to go out looking for a brawl, Daniel. I hope to never have to use it. But if I do have to, I'll be fine. Remember, those idiots at the wedding had machetes and I didn't freeze up."

She thought it was a persuasive point, but he surprised her by laughing.

"Oh, you mean the banditos? Yeah, I'd forgotten all about the armed mercenaries at your wedding. I mean, it happens all the time."

She couldn't suppress her smile. "See?"

He rolled his eyes and then slid back into his all-business teacher persona.

"Well, I'm glad to hear you aren't going to be looking for a knife fight. That weapon is nothing but a hunk of metal wrapped in a big wad of false security. You realize that, right?"

"Yes, in a street fight, it's highly unlikely that I'll have time to draw it," she recited dutifully.

"It's true, you know. I've only ever known one guy who was fast enough to defend himself using a knife."

"Who?"

"My dad."

Larry Steinfeld was a sweet old guy, a retired civil rights and criminal defense attorney, a world-class bridge player, and a lethal weapon in his own right. He'd spent time in the Israeli Army, where he'd learned Krav Maga himself.

"What happened?"

"I don't know the details. You know him, he's pretty low key about his past. But what I do know is instructive. One, he was carrying a sheathed straight blade, like this one. A folding knife is just too slow to get out. And two, he was in close quarters. If you have any distance at all—"

"Run. I know."

"I have to say, I don't know what you're hoping to accomplish by carrying a blade. If you get jumped by someone who's also got a knife, you're much better off disarming him. Turn his own weapon on him. And if your assailant's carrying a gun ... well, you better just hope Leo's nearby with his Glock."

His voice vibrated with frustration.

"I know. Believe me, I agree with everything you're saying. I can't give you any details, but I think Bricker might be planning to come after me in a place where there are a lot of innocent people nearby. If I had to guess, I'd say he'll have a gun. But he's going to have to get pretty close to me to use it without killing a bunch of bystanders. So, what's my play? Let's just walk through it, okay? Gun versus knife in close quarters."

The studio was so quiet she could hear the water from the Chinese restaurant on the first floor running through the pipes. Daniel stared off in the direction of the wall of mirrors, but she could tell he wasn't seeing their reflections. He was absorbed in thought.

When he looked back at her, his face was serious. "Those odds suck."

"Agreed."

She tried to speak lightly but her stomach was clenching.

"And assuming you successfully disarm him, you aren't willing to use the gun against him, right?"

She arched a brow but didn't answer.

"Just checking."

"That's right."

He blew out an exasperated breath, ruffling his brown hair. "Okay. Put that down and let's block it out."

She returned the knife to its sheath and joined him on the mats.

"Your best, and as far as I can see, only advantage in gun versus knife is going to be speed." As he warmed to the topic, he began to bounce lightly on the balls of his bare feet. "I think one of the police departments did a study and concluded that the average attacker could cover something like seven yards in a second and a half."

She grinned at his encyclopedic grasp of law-enforcement-related research. He shared her near-photographic memory. The only difference was that he used his to catalog combat and self-defense information, while she put hers to work filing away legal precedents and the facts central to various client disputes.

"That's fast."

"It is, but you have to be faster. Assuming your fake military leader has any training, he'll be following the rule of thumb that his zone of danger is twenty-one feet. He'll want to shoot you at about ten yards out, if he can."

She focused on the details of what he was

saying to avoid reflecting on the chilling larger topic."

"Why ten yards?"

"Even someone with a lot of firearms training will be hard-pressed to get two rounds off in less time than it takes to cover thirty feet. You should ask Leo how fast he can draw and shoot his weapon with reasonable accuracy. It takes longer than you'd think."

"I will. So let's do this." She rolled her shoulders and assumed a neutral position.

He tilted his head. "No, actually. I think the highest and best use of your time would be to spend it working on your speed, especially your fast-twitch muscles."

"I'm pretty fast."

"You are. But you need to be blazingly fast. You know what that means?"

"Not suicides."

"Yes, suicides."

He gave her a look that shut down any objections she might have raised.

"Fine." She huffed as she walked to the edge of the studio, not even bothering to keep the sullen note out of her voice.

He ignored her pouting and focused on his stopwatch.

She dropped into a runner's stance. The fingertips of her right hand grazed the end of the mat.

"And ... Go!"

She pushed off with an explosive motion and sprinted to the far edge of the mat, touched it, turned and raced back to where she'd begun. She brushed the mat and turned again, this time running to the far edge of the second mat, repeated the touch-and-turn sequence, and ran back to the starting position. Her lungs were already burning. She worked up some saliva in her mouth, and raced to the edge of the third mat and returned. As she ran to the fourth and final mat, Daniel shouted, "Turn it on!"

Turn it on? Did he think she was jogging over here?

She dug deeper and found a final burst of speed. She reached the edge of the mat and bent, her hand dangling loosely over the mat, then she turned and raced back to the start.

Daniel stopped the timer.

"Not bad."

"Not bad? How long?" she panted.

"Doesn't matter. You didn't touch the mat that last time, so it doesn't count. Do it again."

She stared at him as she sucked down great gulps of air. He was right, she had missed the mat. She'd hoped he hadn't noticed. No such luck.

"Get ready."

"Now? C'mon, give me a minute."

"No. Get on the line."

She bit her lip and dropped to a starting position. Her hair was heavy against her hot neck and she would have loved to take a sip of water, but she knew he was right. Shaving even half a second off her time could save her life.

"Go!"

She ran.

23

Sasha carried the last of her bags up the steep stairs leading into the rented Victorian. Leo reasoned it must have been the one filled with dozens of pairs of ridiculous high heels. She seemed to be struggling under its weight, but he knew better than to offer to help.

She didn't take kindly to any gesture that might be interpreted as questioning her strength. And, more relevant here, he'd made the mild observation when she was packing that she probably didn't need to bring quite so many shoes. She hadn't responded verbally, but he could still feel the sting of the death-ray that had shot from her eyes.

No, this was not a time for chivalry; this was a time for self-preservation.

She passed him on the stairs empty-handed, on her way back to the car for another armload.

"Where's Java?" he asked.

"He's under the couch. All the noise is scaring him. Naya's going to try to lure him out with some milk. All that's left is the coffee grinder."

"I'll get it."

She turned and offered him a genuine smile. "I don't think so. That's my favorite wedding present. If you drop it, I'll have to divorce you."

He laughed, more at the humor in her green eyes than at her lame joke.

She stopped. "I know this kind of sucks, but we can make the best of it."

"I know. You're like cheese."

"Pardon?"

"Cheese. Everything's better with cheese. And everything's better with you."

She rolled her eyes and continued on her way. He thought her step seemed a little lighter.

She was right. They could make the best of it. It might even be fun. They'd enjoyed babysitting her nieces and nephews.

Living with six kids would be just like babysitting for a few hours. Or maybe not.

He walked through the front door of his temporary new home with his arms full of bags and stopped just inside to survey the damage. The place looked like a Toys R Us had exploded.

He exhaled slowly and caught Cole's eye.

"Can you give me a hand with this stuff? There's more out on the porch."

Cole nodded and untangled himself from his youngest sister's grasp. She was wrapped around his neck and back. He deposited her on the couch and trotted out of the room.

"Good thing you're here," Cole said. "Naya seems to be at her limit."

Naya, her head under the couch, apparently still engaged in her cat-retrieval efforts, yelled, "I heard that."

"See?"

Leo clasped the boy's shoulder in solidarity. Sasha in a bad mood was like a storm. Naya in a bad mood was like a tropical superstorm.

As soon as they stepped out on to the porch, the boy's face grew serious.

"It's also a good thing you're here because I need to talk to you. Both of you." He jerked his head toward Sasha, who was approaching them with a two-hundred dollar burr grinder lovingly cradled in her arms.

"What's going on?" she asked, taking in the boy's somber expression. "Is Java stuck?"

"No. Listen. I didn't want to worry Naya but while you were gone, she ran out real quick to get some groceries."

"You guys are out of food again *already?*" Sasha looked personally affronted that her provisions hadn't lasted longer.

"Yeah, anyway. She'd been gone a while and the doorbell rang. I figured her arms were full so I opened it and—"

"You *opened* it?"

The boy's eyes widened at the note of squeaky outrage in Sasha's voice, and he looked at Leo for support.

"Um, yeah. I know I should have confirmed it was her first, but I didn't. Okay? Anyway, it wasn't Naya. It was some dude holding a clipboard and a package."

"A delivery person?"

"No. I mean, not like UPS or Fed Ex. He wasn't wearing any kind of uniform, so I got kind of nervous. I started to close the door on him and he reached out real fast and caught it. He knew my name—"

"Which name?" Sasha asked. "Did he call you Cole or Clay?"

"My name's *not* Clay anymore." He forced the words out between clenched teeth.

“Okay, sorry. Go on.”

“He asked if I was Cole Bennett. I said ‘who wants to know?’ He didn’t say who he was or what he wanted. He just asked if I was eighteen years old and I said no, then I grabbed the door and slammed it shut and locked it.”

The boy’s face was white as he remembered the interaction.

“You did good, Cole,” Leo assured him.

He shook his head in disagreement. “No, I never should have opened the door. Who was it? It was the feds, right? They’re going to split us up or put us in a foster home, aren’t they?”

Leo cleared his throat to buy time.

“I don’t know, Cole. I doubt it. Hank didn’t tell anyone from Witness Protection your exact location—”

“Where is Hank, anyway?” The kid rocked back on his heels.

“He had a meeting. But I really doubt that whoever it was came from the government.”

Leo could feel Sasha’s eyes on his back cautioning him not to say too much. He probably already had, but he wanted to ease the boy’s mind. He didn’t know who was trying to track down Cole Bennett, but he was fairly certain it wasn’t WITSEC.

Now, who it *was*—that was the question.

Cole's breathing slowed. "Oh. Yeah, I guess they know I'm not eighteen, anyway."

"That's true," Leo agreed.

"Well then who do you think it was?"

"I have no idea. Could have been anyone—a pollster, a door-to-door marketer. I don't know."

"I guess. Okay, sorry for overreacting." The boy said the words slowly, as if he weren't quite convinced that there was no reason to panic. But he couldn't identify one, so it seemed as if he would let it go.

"Don't apologize. You're smart to be cautious."

His mother's murder hung in the air between them.

Leo could tell they were both thinking that if Anna had been a little more careful, she might still be alive.

"Uh ... okay. Thanks."

The boy smiled weakly and walked back into the house.

Leo started to follow him, but Sasha yanked him back onto the porch one-handed. She'd tucked the grinder into the crook of her elbow.

"What?"

She stared at him.

"What? What do you think? You know who that was, right?"

"At the door?"

"Yes, at the door."

"No, like I told Cole, I have no idea ..." He trailed off.

He really didn't know who it could be, but he didn't think it was a federal agent. He shielded his eyes from the late afternoon sun and waited for her to tell him what she thought.

She gave him a look of disbelief. "Connelly, I'm sure it was a process server."

He cocked his head.

"Pulaski probably wants Cole to testify," she explained.

"He wants him to testify on behalf of Bricker? That's insane."

"No." She corrected him with a vigorous shake of her head. Her loose wavy hair fell over her face and she pushed it aside. "It's not insane. It's ballsy and inappropriate. In other words, it's right out of Andy Pulaski's play book."

"There's no way Pulaski could have tracked down the kids, Sasha."

Even as he said it, he realized the fallacy of the statement. There was *always* a way to track someone down—unless the person you were tracking was in Witness Protection, of course. He swallowed a bitter laugh.

"Believe what you want. I'm telling you. The process server asked if he was eighteen because service of a subpoena wouldn't be valid if he gave it to a minor. Pulaski may not know how old Cole is, but he knows where he is. I know it."

Leo shivered. He looked up to see if a cloud had passed over the hot May sun. One hadn't.

Sasha looked at him, her green eyes deep pools of worry.

"It's going to be okay. And I know you don't agree with this, but I've been thinking—I should be carrying."

She shook her head. "Please don't bring your gun into the house with all these kids here."

He grabbed her wrist. "Sasha—"

"Anyway, you don't need it. I have a knife."

She squeezed his hand and crossed the threshold into the house, leaving him to stand in the doorway and blink in disbelief.

Sasha had armed herself? She was more shaken than she'd let on.

He stood on the porch for a long moment. Then he slowly took the steps back down to the street, his heart hammering in his chest. He unlocked the SUV's passenger door and then unlocked the glove compartment.

He took out his Glock and turned it over in his hands, then he glanced up at the house and holstered the gun.

His wife had to trust her instincts, and he had to trust his.

24

Andy Pulaski rubbed his forehead. He'd wasted a hundred bucks hiring a private investigator to follow Sasha McCandless' paralegal on a hunch that she'd lead him to the kids.

The hunch had paid off, but the PI said the oldest kid wasn't yet eighteen so he hadn't served him.

In retrospect, of course, he should have figured. The stupid irrevocable trust was for the benefit of the *minor* children, but it was worth sending up a flyer to see if maybe the oldest kid had turned eighteen since it had been drafted.

Of course, he didn't dare submit the expense to that old hag Perry-Brown for reimbursement. He could almost hear her crowing, 'Do you know the meaning of minor, Mr. Pulaski?'

Forget the benjamin, Big Gun, focus.

After his initial annoyance at having been appointed to represent some in-the-wind, prepper freak, he'd calmed down and realized this pain-in-the-butt court appointment could be his golden goose.

He just had to play it right.

If he could get Judge Perry-Brown to rule that it was in the Bennett kids' best interests to maintain contact with their father, it would be a stunning victory. A career maker. He'd solidify himself as the go-to guy for fathers with ugly stories but big bank accounts.

But with no client around to tell his story, and no access to the kids, how exactly was he supposed to overcome the bias against Bricker?

Not to mention the unfortunate fact that Bricker's estranged wife had been brutally murdered while he was on the run.

A lesser attorney than Sasha McCandless could spin this story into a nightmare, and, unfortunately, for all her deceptive cuteness, she was a nasty bulldog. She was going to pummel him. Unless he came up with something good. And fast.

He drummed his fingers on his desk and reread his notes.

How to make Bricker sympathetic?

His mind was a perfect blank. He'd represented some unlikeable people, but this guy really took the cake.

He balled up his notes and threw them in the wastebasket.

He was sitting at his desk, staring at nothing, when the telephone rang. He ignored it.

A moment later, Becca, his secretary, appeared in the doorway.

"Andy?"

"What?"

"I'm sorry to bother you. There's a Mr. Bricker on the phone."

Andy's head snapped back.

"Did you say Bricker?"

"That's the name he gave. Isn't that your absentee dad?"

"Put him through." He waved her away.

"Sure." She pulled the door shut behind her.

He pressed his hands against the top of his desk and steadied his breathing.

The transfer tone sounded and the red light on his telephone blinked up at him.

He exhaled and hit the speaker button.

"What can I do for you, Mr. Bricker?" he said with all the bravado he could muster.

"It's more a matter of what you *will* do for me, Big Gun." Bricker's voice crackled in his ear.

Andy told himself the chill he felt was anticipation, not fear.

"And what would that be?"

Bricker was silent for a beat.

Then he said, "I understand you've been appointed to represent me in a proceeding to terminate my parental rights. Is that correct?"

"Yes. How did you—?"

"That's not your concern."

"I'm not so sure about that. But, regardless, I assume you object to any termination?"

Andy swiveled his desk chair around and propped his feet up on his windowsill. He imagined his view was of something other than the strip mall's dumpsters.

"You assume wrong. I hardly think I'm in any position to take custody of my children, given my … circumstances."

"Oh."

Andy's feet thudded to the floor, and his shoulders sagged.

"So, you want to consent?"

His golden goose was turning into a chicken.

"With caveats. One, I want my children to be freed."

"Freed?"

"The government is holding them hostage. That's unconscionable, wouldn't you say?"

"Mm-hmm."

Great, just great. Bricker was sticking to his anti-government craziness.

"Two, I do not consent to the appointment of Sasha McCandless as trustee. I don't want her anywhere near my kids."

"Uh, so you want to contest the will but not the termination of your rights?"

"Is that a problem?"

"Kind of. I only represent you for the purposes of the rights termination hearing."

Silence on the line.

"Can I retain you to contest the will?"

"You could, but to be candid, you shouldn't."

"Why's that?"

"It's not what I do."

"Are you a big gun or not?" Bricker barked.

Despite himself, Andy snapped to attention.

"Yes, sir."

"Then act like it. I want Sasha McCandless and the federal government out of my children's lives. Period."

"Who do you want to take care of them?" Andy asked, mainly out of curiosity.

"I don't care. Just as long as it's not the feds or that whore lawyer."

"Ooooo-kay. Well, I should get you a retainer agreement, and we need to discuss my fee—"

"I don't care about the minutiae. Do what I say and you'll be compensated."

Andy wasn't inclined to argue. He glanced down at his phone's display. *Private caller.*

"How do I get in touch with you?"

"You don't."

More silence.

Andy listened to his watch ticking and the building's rattling HVAC system for half a minute, then he said, "Are you going to want to know what's going on in the case?"

"When did the judge set the hearing for the rights termination?"

"Day after tomorrow. Ten a.m."

"Friday? That's awfully short notice, isn't it?"

Andy barked out a bitter laugh. "I'll say. But since you're in the wind, the judge used her discretion to determine that making McCandless comply with the notice provision would be futile."

"Can she do that?"

"The judge? She can do anything she wants."

Bricker grunted. "I'll call you at noon after the hearing."

Before he could respond, a loud click sounded in his ear.

Andy dropped the earpiece back into its cradle, wheeled his chair around, and contemplated his non-view once more. A slow smile spread across his face.

If this went well, his next window would look out on the city skyline not the trash bins.

25

"What's she doing?" Brianna asked, threading her fingers through the wire diamond pattern covering the fence that enclosed the basketball court, separating it from the playground. She nodded toward the court.

"Who? Sasha?" Leo asked.

"Duh."

What she was *trying* to do was tire out the Bennett family so they'd sleep soundly.

After a dinner of tacos that had left a mess on the floor that really called for a wet/dry vac rather than a broom, she'd suggested they all walk down to the neighborhood playground. The Bennetts, however, appeared to be indefatigable.

He turned his attention away from Mark, who

was trying to give him a heart attack by racing Hal and Calla around on an old metal merry-go-round with all his might. As the little ones swung wildly, they shrieked with joy. Leo's reflexive shout of 'hold on!' with every orbit they made only increased their enjoyment.

He followed the girl's gaze to the blacktop, where Leah and Cole had been playing one-on-one the last time he'd looked. Now they were standing on the midcourt line watching Sasha gesture from one end of the court to the other. Leah balanced the basketball on her hip and wore a skeptical look. Cole was grinning broadly.

"I'm not sure," Leo admitted.

Sasha crouched and touched the line with her fingertips then resumed her vigorous pointing.

"Oh. Wait, I know. She's teaching them how to do suicides."

The girl turned and faced him full-on, her eyes enormous in her freckled face. "Suicides?"

"Suicide sprints," he assured her. "It's a conditioning drill for runners."

"Why are they called suicides?"

"I guess because you feel like you're dying when you're done. Some people also call them ladders or blood and guts. But suicides is pretty accurate."

She wrinkled her nose. "Then why do them?"

"They help you build speed. It looks like your brother and sister are going to give it a try. Wanna join them?"

"No. Way." She stretched her two-word response into two sentences.

Sasha jogged to the far out of bounds line, trailed by Cole and Leah. The three dropped into a runner's stance and toed the line.

"She's going to run, too?" Brianna asked.

"Looks like it."

"Weird."

"Bet she wins."

"No. Chance." Briana bugged her eyes out at him as if she couldn't believe her ears.

"Sasha's pretty fast."

"Cole is super fast. Plus, she's old ... and a girl."

Leo sent a silent message of gratitude up to the heavens that Sasha hadn't been close enough to hear the comment. He wasn't sure which part would irritate her more—the knock on her age or the one on her gender—but he was certain the remark would not have passed unnoticed.

"Yeah? I think she's faster."

The girl gaped at him. "You're banana cakes."

He assumed banana cakes meant crazy.

"Want to wager?"

"Like bet on them?"

"Exactly. If Cole wins, I'll take you all out for ice cream."

"What if Sasha wins?"

He flashed her a grin. "*She'll* take you all out for ice cream. You in?"

"Well, duh!"

On the court, Sasha held up her hand to indicate they were about to start. The instant she dropped her hand, brother and sister burst off the line, running at full speed. Cole quickly pulled ahead by a stride, and Sasha trailed Leah by an equal measure.

"See?" Brianna gloated.

"Just wait."

The kids were running flat out. They would have nothing left in reserve when Sasha poured it on. They hit the first line, and Sasha caught up with Cole. At the second line, she was a half-step ahead of him. Before the third, Leah was flagging well behind and panting hard.

Mark abandoned the merry-go-round. He and the youngest two joined Leo and Brianna at the fence.

"Run, Cole! You can catch her!" Brianna shouted.

"Go, Cole, go!" Hal and Calla chanted, bouncing up and down in their excitement.

The commotion caught Sasha's attention. She glanced over and winked.

Then Leo watched as she dug in and found a final pocket of speed somewhere within. She rocketed forward. Her long hair streamed behind her. Her arms and legs were a blur of motion.

Cole didn't let up, but there was no catching her.

She hit the final line and touched it two-handed then waited for Cole and Leah to cross it. She high-fived each of them.

They headed toward the fence. Sasha had her arms over her head, trying to catch her breath.

"I feel like I'm gonna barf," Leah announced as they approached.

Leo shot Brianna a look that said 'see?'

Brianna nodded sagely. "Suicides."

"Your wife is tough," Cole informed him.

You don't know the half of it, Leo thought.

"Tell me about it," he said.

Sasha beamed. "I had some stiff competition."

"And you get to buy us all ice cream now!" Brianna exclaimed.

"I do?"

"You do," Leo confirmed. "I won a bet."

"Well lucky you. Tell you what, since I'm paying, we'll get frozen yogurt."

A series of muffled groans sounded among the siblings. Sasha waved them off.

"Trust me. You're going to love it. There's a topping bar the length of the store. You can get every kind of candy imaginable to put on top."

"Even gummi worms?" Calla asked, narrowing her eyes.

"Especially gummi worms," Sasha promised.

"Yay!"

The girl leapt at Sasha, who just managed to catch her.

Over the top of Calla's mop of hair, Sasha caught Leo's eyes and grinned.

She looked so happy and so natural holding the small girl in her arms that his breath caught in his throat.

26

Thursday

Sasha moaned and tried to turn onto her side, shielding her eyes from the sunlight that streamed through the slatted blinds. "Youch."

"Are you okay?" Connelly whispered.

She uncovered one eye to look at him. "No."

She raised her head to plump up her pillow, but every part of her body was stiff. She collapsed back onto the bed and her unplumped pillow.

"What's wrong? Are you sore from your race last night?" he teased.

"Something like that."

Sore from the race and the twelve sets of suicides Daniel had made her run earlier in the day.

"Well it was worth it. You have a whole fan club now."

He reached across the bed and pulled her close.

"I think that's due more to the eighty-seven pounds of frozen yogurt than my sprinting prowess."

"I think it's both."

She grinned into his chest.

She'd had a lot of fun with him and the kids the night before. More fun than she'd had in a long time, her screaming muscles notwithstanding.

She snuggled in closer for an early morning cuddle and felt his body yielding to hers. And then cabinet doors banged downstairs.

She hauled her aching body to an upright position.

"What's wrong?" he asked, switching from languid to alert in an instant.

"We have to go down there and parent—or at least supervise," she informed him, pulling on a sweatshirt over her thin t-shirt and shorts.

"What? They're fine."

He tried to pull her back into bed, but she shook him off.

"You don't know that. Hal could be trying to cook eggs. Or Leah could be standing on top of the island again trying to reach the granola bars. Come on."

He groaned but swung his legs over the edge of the bed and raised his arms in a stretch.

"Fine."

She stopped in the doorway and looked back.

"Hey, before we walk into the circus, I wanted to ask you something."

"Yeah? I wanted to ask you something, too," he said.

"Oh. Okay. You first," she said. She leaned against the door frame.

Connelly sat up straighter and pierced her with his almond-shaped eyes, which were suddenly alert and devoid of any sleepiness.

"Come here." He patted the bed.

She walked over uncertainly.

"What's up?" she asked as she perched beside him.

"What are your current thoughts about having kids?"

She blinked.

"Um..."

Before she could formulate an answer, he pressed on. "Not a baby. Kids. Those kids downstairs tearing the kitchen apart."

Her head felt cloudy, full of cotton. "You mean adopt them?"

"Yes." His voice was clear and strong, full of conviction.

"Uh—" she cast around for a response. "To be completely honest, Connelly, the thought never crossed my mind."

"That's okay. Will you think about it, though?" He smiled widely at her, his eyes shining with excitement at the idea.

"Sure. Yes. I'll give it a lot of thought."

He kissed the top of her head.

"Thank you. Now what did you want to talk about?"

"What? Oh. Nothing really. I was just wondering ..."

"Yeah?"

She winced at the sharp change in subjects as she posed her question. "I was just wondering how long it would take you to get off two accurate shots with your Glock."

He blinked.

"Why?"

A crash sounded from the kitchen.

"That sounded like glass breaking. We can talk about it later."

She sprinted out of the room and down the stairs.

27

Sasha looked around the cramped breakfast nook, which Hank had commandeered as a conference room. Will was sitting ramrod straight with his hands suspended inches above the table, as though he were a marionette awaiting his puppet master.

She swiped one of the napkins from the Jake's takeout tray that Naya had balanced on top of a half-constructed Lego village and mopped up the sticky puddle of orange juice pooling in front of him.

He smiled gratefully.

"Sorry for the ambiance, guys, but Hank insisted we meet here and not at the office. So it's your party," Sasha said, turning the meeting over to

Hank, who was squeezed into a kid-sized chair that Connelly had dragged in from the playroom.

She sipped her to-go coffee and waited.

"Right. In light of yesterday's visitor, it's time to go to the mattresses." Hank imbued the sentence with a grave undertone.

Naya caught her eye and threw her a quizzical look.

Sasha shrugged. *No idea*, she mouthed.

Connelly watched the exchange with a grin.

He leaned forward and stage whispered, "You two are pathetic. Pick up some Godfather DVDs already. It means we're at war. When mafia families are about to start a war, they send their foot soldiers to safe houses. They sleep on mattresses on the floor."

Sasha rolled her eyes. Hank and Connelly and their love for Godfather quotes would never cease to baffle her.

Naya seemed similarly unimpressed. "How dramatic. Aren't we already in a safe house?"

"No. If Sasha's right, Bricker's lawyer managed to find this place without much difficulty. We have to assume anyone who's been properly motivated could do the same. Not to mention, I still don't know how Bricker found them down in North Carolina. I was as careful as possible in making this move, but there's no guarantee one of my men isn't a leaker."

Connelly's eyebrow nearly shot off his forehead.

"I doubt that very much, Hank."

"I doubt it, too. But I'm not willing to gamble six lives on being right. Are you?"

Hank looked around the table. No one else spoke for a long moment.

Finally, Will cleared his throat. "Surely you can get WITSEC to assign around-the-clock protection. If you hand-pick the team and the five of us take turns supervising the marshals, we can be fairly certain that there are no more leaks and the children are safe. It seems like it would be an unnecessary stressor to uproot them again."

Sasha kept her face a neutral mask. She never would have expected Will to volunteer for babysitting duty. He was just full of surprises.

"It may be a stressor," Hank agreed, "but I'm afraid it's very necessary. My meeting here and the follow-up session in D.C. did not go well."

Will sat up straighter. "Oh? How so?"

Hank squeezed his eyes shut and pinched the bridge of his nose for several seconds before answering. "To make a very long and infuriating story short, the Bennett children have been terminated from the witness protection program, effective immediately. In fact, in reliance on a legal opinion provided by counsel to Homeland Security, their termination is retroactively backdated to the day Allison died."

"What?" Will sputtered. "That's outrageous."

"Agreed," Hank said flatly.

Connelly frowned. "Why was Homeland Security weighing in? Isn't this a Justice issue?"

"One would think. The Department of Justice attorneys shared your view—until some middle manager realized that letting ICE and Homeland Security take the lead would make Allison Bennett's death a national security issue. As a result, the investigation would be shrouded in secrecy and the results never made public."

"So?" Naya asked.

"So WITSEC can continue to claim they've never lost a witness who followed the rules."

Sasha felt her neck snap back in surprise. "They're saying Allison Bennett broke the rules?"

Hank answered in a mechanical voice. "There is currently no evidence that Allison Bennett's killer knew her or, more important, knew that she was the former Anna Bricker. The official viewpoint is that she was the unfortunate victim of a home invasion."

"A home invasion in Sunnyvale, North Carolina?"

"Correct." Hank either didn't notice or had no answer for the disbelief dripping from Naya's voice. "And, given the fact that her minor children were not themselves witnesses in the federal case against their father, said minor children are neither entitled nor required to remain in the program after her untimely death. To compound the situation, WITSEC is viewing their contact with me—and our subsequent involvement in their care—as evidence that the children have failed to abide by the rules."

Sasha suddenly felt cold. The outcome was no surprise, given Connelly's report of their initial meeting with WITSEC, but the government's dispassionate ability to throw six innocent children out on their ears was chilling all the same.

"And Homeland Security figures into this how, exactly?" Will wanted to know.

Hank managed a bitter laugh. "Although there's no evidence Jeffrey Bricker played a role in his estranged wife's death, he *is* a would-be terrorist, a convicted murderer, and an escaped felon. Any battle involving custody of his children would obviously be viewed through the lens on its impact on national security."

"Obviously," Sasha echoed, even though that convoluted reasoning was anything but obvious.

"And if Bricker finds his kids and murders them?" Connelly whispered furiously.

"Officially not WITSEC's problem."

She could tell from the expressions on the faces around the table that this turn of events was making everyone feel the way she felt—unsettled, slightly nauseous, and jittery.

"Okay," she said slowly. "Hank's right. We've got to move them."

"No way," said a firm voice from the doorway.

Five heads turned toward the sound. And there stood Cole, red-faced, his hands balled into fists, and his back ramrod straight.

"We're not going anywhere," he said.

Great.

They'd been so focused on Hank's news, no one had noticed the boy creep into the room.

Sasha and Connelly exchanged a look. Someone had to diffuse the situation. Judging by the encouraging nod Connelly gave her, she was that someone.

Even better.

"How long have you been standing there?" she asked.

"Long enough." He stiffened even more.

She walked over to join him near the hallway. She didn't dare reach out and touch him. He was shaking with rage.

"Listen," she said in a low voice, "I understand. I really do."

It was the exactly wrong thing to say.

He stared at her with dark, warning eyes and hissed, "No, you don't. None of you know what it's like for us!"

He turned and ran toward the front of the house.

"Cole, no! Wait!" Connelly shouted.

Sasha threw him an apologetic look and sprinted after the boy.

By the time she hit the front porch, he was already halfway down the block.

She ran down the stairs with ease, thankful both for her running workouts on Pittsburgh's various sets of crumbling city-owned steps and for the fact that for once she was wearing flats instead of stilettos. The fleeting thought crossed her mind that, given the frequency with which she found herself sprinting, it might be time to retire high heels from her wardrobe for good.

Bite your tongue, she told herself.

She ran harder, closing the distance between her and the boy.

He reached the corner and hesitated, glancing over his shoulder at her, then spun wildly and ran to his left, toward the small community garden and park that anchored the neighborhood.

She had to catch him before he reached the edge of the park. It backed up to acres of undeveloped woods, filled with junk, poison ivy, and who knew what else.

She dug in and increased her speed.

Cole slowed to a jog and then a walk. He stopped beside the raised box holding tidy rows of cornstalks and leaned on the chicken wire that protected it from the local rabbits.

She came to a stop and stood a few feet away, trying to decide if she should move closer or give him his space.

His narrow shoulders heaved. Even though his back was to her, she could tell he was sobbing.

She walked over and wrapped her arms around his shoulders. She had to stretch on her toes to reach him. He was so tall, half boy and half man.

He wiped his eyes with the back of his hand but didn't shake her off. She hugged him tighter.

"Hey, it's okay to cry, you know."

"No, it's not. I have to be strong. We're all alone now. And I'm in charge." His voice was thick with tears and muffled by his hands.

"That's not true. Look at me, Cole."

He swallowed hard and raised his red-rimmed eyes to meet her gaze.

"Yeah?" he sniffed.

"Yeah. I guess you heard that the government is kicking you guys out of witness protection. I can't defend that action. But I promise you this, those people sitting around the table, they're not going to abandon you. And neither am I. Okay?"

He nodded slowly. "Okay."

"Okay. So, you don't need to be strong. What you need to be is a kid."

"No, I need a seat at the table. It's only fair. You're making decisions that impact my family." He jutted out his chin and stared at her defiantly, waiting for her to object.

She studied him and considered her response.

"I'll make it happen. In return, you'll be mindful of the danger you're in. No more running off. Deal?"

She stuck out her hand.

He smiled and pumped it.

"Deal."

"Good," she said, throwing an arm around his shoulder. "Especially since you should know by now, you're never going to outrun me, kid. I'm like the wind."

He laughed reluctantly. "Right."

"Come on. We need to get back before Hank pulls a brain muscle worrying."

His chuckle turned into a real laugh as they headed back toward the house.

SASHA RETURNED WITH COLE, and the group reassembled at the table.

This time, Naya bowed out to fix sandwiches for the kids' lunch.

Cole took her seat.

To Leo's eternal amusement, Hank stayed sandwiched in the kid-sized chair. His arms and legs jack-knifed and folded.

Leo leaned back, stretching his legs in his luxurious adult-sized chair, and watched as the teenager set out the reasons why he thought they should stay in the house. He was articulate and passionate, but Leo could tell that Will and Hank were unmoved by his argument.

"Son," Will finally interrupted, "I understand what you're saying. Your brothers and sisters have been through a great deal, no one disputes that. And you have, too. But if you want to be treated as an adult, you need to hear the very adult reality:

there's a good chance your father's going to come after you. And, if not you, then Sasha and Leo. If he learns where you are, and where they are, your entire family will be in danger. If WITSEC were in the picture, staying put might be a risk worth taking. But they aren't, so it's not."

Leo was impressed by Will's cool logic, but the kid wasn't swayed.

"Am I supposed to run from that dirtbag for the rest of my life?" he countered.

"No, you're not. I'm going to stop him and put him back where he belongs: behind bars," Hank intoned. "But until I do, I need to know that you're all safe."

Cole said nothing but set his mouth in a hard line.

Leo glanced over at Sasha, but she was distracted by her phone on her lap. It looked like she was texting or emailing someone. She wasn't going to be any help.

"Listen," he interjected, "what if you help find a new place? I mean, Hank got this house because it was the first thing he could find, he had access to it through his sources, and it's better than nothing. But why don't you talk to your brothers and sisters and come up with a wish list—for instance, Leah would probably like a nice, level backyard where she can garden. I know she still has some more of your mom's seeds left. Anyway, you guys can come up with some ideas about location, size, features, whatever. And then we can work together to find something that truly fits your needs. How's that sound?"

The boy's jaw softened. "That would be good, yeah."

It was Hank's turn to frown. "Fine. But time's of the essence here. We can't dilly-dally. Go ahead and talk to them and start packing up. We need to move out by tomorrow evening at the absolute latest. If we have to stay in motels short term while you're looking for a new place, we will. But we can't stay here."

"Understood. And thanks." Cole nodded seriously and went off in search of his siblings.

"He's being forced to grow up too fast," Leo said as he watched the boy disappear.

Beside him, Sasha made a soft *hmm* noise but didn't look up from her Blackberry.

Irritation pricked at his neck. Couldn't she put down her stupid phone and stop messing around with work emails for one day? Caroline was at the office covering all the phones.

He huffed out a loud, dramatic sigh intended to draw her attention.

When she looked up, her eyes were wide with fear, and his annoyance vanished instantly.

"Sorry, were you saying something?"

She tried to cover up her concern, but he knew her too well. Sasha was afraid.

He reached over to take her hand. Just then, Naya appeared in the doorway with a tray of turkey sandwiches in one hand and a triumphant smile plastered on her face.

"I think I know how Bricker found Allison," she said.

At the exact same moment, Sasha blurted, "Someone broke into the condo."

After a heavy silence, everyone started talking at once.

Will held up a hand and took control of the chaos.

"Hang on. Let's do one thing at a time." He turned to Sasha. "What happened at your condo?"

She took a long, centering breath. "Maisy was getting ready to head out for a lunch date. As she walked down the hallway, she noticed that the door to my place ... I mean, our place ... was ajar. She peeked her head in to say hi and she said the place is trashed." She glanced at Leo with an unreadable expression.

"Anything missing?" he asked.

"She wouldn't know. She called 9-1-1 and canceled on her date to wait until the cops get there. I'd like to be there when they arrive."

She blanched, and he knew she was thinking of her client files.

Hank cleared his throat. "Is your gun secure?"

Leo patted his waistband. "It's on me."

"Good."

He felt Sasha's eyes on him but didn't meet her gaze. They could fight about the gun later.

"Is Maisy okay to stay there?" Naya asked, a worried crease wrinkling her forehead.

"She said the place was empty. I told her to stay outside, just in case. I doubt she searched it thoroughly."

Sasha scooped up her keys, phone, and wallet and dumped them all into her bag. Leo noted with relief that her hands were steady now. Then he looked down at his own and willed himself to stop their trembling.

"You coming?" she said.

"Yes." He stood to follow her. "Wait, Naya had an epiphany."

Naya waved them toward the door. "Never mind that. Good news always keeps. Go."

But Will shook his head. "No. If you have a

theory as to how Bricker found his family, it could be important."

"Critical, even," Hank added.

Sasha paused in the doorway to hear what Naya had to say, but Leo could feel the impatience radiating off her in waves. He gave her what he hoped was a soothing smile.

"Okay, well, as I was slicing tomatoes for the sandwiches, it dawned on me."

"What dawned on you?" Sasha asked, hurrying her along.

"The seeds. Fly Boy over there mentioned using some of Allison's seeds to start a garden at the new house when the kids move."

"Right, Leah has this stainless steel container full of seeds she brought with her when they moved. I helped her plant some out back because they had to leave their mom's garden behind," Leo volunteered.

Her voice gathered strength and confidence as she went on. "Exactly. So I took a look at the seed vault."

"And?"

"And remember how I connected Celia Gerig to the preppers?" Naya asked professorially.

Suddenly he could imagine her in court, authoritative and convincing, persuading a jury to find for her client. But he couldn't recall the Gerig connection. "Sorry, not really."

"I do," Sasha interjected. "She was asking about heirloom seeds on some message board."

"Bingo! And who do you think responded with a link to a recommendation? Your girl, Anna Bricker. I pulled up the cached page. The company she told Celia to use is the same one that made the canister in the mudroom."

"How on earth did you remember that?" Will asked, impressed but baffled.

"Hey. Mac's not the only one with a steel trap for a memory."

Sasha smiled. "So how do you think that leads to Bricker exactly?"

"Figure a year and a half has passed. Bricker's behind bars. Allison and the kids have a new life, no one knows where they are. She decides she wants a garden. She knows it's a theoretical risk to order from this survivalist company she's done business with in the past. But their product's superior and the price is right. She rationalizes it and places an order under her new name. When Bricker gets out, he starts trying to track her down. He hits dead end after dead end until he remembers the seed company. He contacts the company and gets a list of everyone who ordered seeds for this planting season. Alphabetical list? Allison Bennett, Anna Bricker? It wouldn't take a genius to connect the dots. And anyway, he sort of is one."

"Okay. Sure, that's plausible. It's a stretch, but Bricker presumably knew her as well as anybody, if not better. If gardening was her thing, he could have predicted her habits." Sasha glanced at Hank. "Would it be breaking any WITSEC rules to order from a company that you've done business with in the past—I mean, using the new name?"

He frowned. "Not exactly. But witnesses are encouraged to break ties with their old lives. It wouldn't take much for some overeager junior attorney who heard Naya's theory to chalk Allison's death up to her carelessness."

Will twisted his mouth into a sour knot, leaving no room for doubt as to how he felt about such an argument, even in the hypothetical.

After a moment, he smoothed his expression into a smile and reached over to pat Naya on the shoulder. "Very nice work, Naya."

Leo could have sworn he saw her blush—her dark skin turned momentarily dusky.

She ducked her head and said, "It was nothing, really. I was just spit balling. I'm probably totally off-base. Anyway, I should get these sandwiches into the kids' bellies before they get *hangry*."

Leo laughed. The younger ones, especially, did seem to become extraordinarily cranky if their meals and snacks were spaced too far apart. It kind of reminded him of his bride, to be honest.

But Sasha stopped Naya in her tracks.

"Wait. Don't do that."

"Don't feed the kids?"

"No. Don't brush off a compliment, ever. But especially don't brush off a compliment about your legal acumen." Sasha's eyes were smiling but her tone was anything but light.

"Oh-kay?"

"Listen, there will be plenty of people who will be more than happy to denigrate or minimize your achievements. Believe me. Eight years working for Prescott taught me that much, if nothing else. Don't help them out by selling yourself short. Will's right. You had a great insight. He recognized it. The proper response is a simple thank you."

"Okay, okay," Naya mumbled.

Sasha stuck a hand on her hip and cocked her head toward Will.

Naya glared for a moment then turned and said, "Thank you, Will."

"You're quite welcome." He punctuated the words with a formal little bob of his head.

"Happy now?" she asked Sasha.

"Yes. Now go feed the wild things before they eat each other up."

The two shared some secret woman smile for a second.

Sasha turned to Leo. "Come on. Let's go rescue Maisy from the crime scene."

"Ha. Rescue her? She's probably working on her pitch to get the exclusive interview as we speak."

28

Bricker gathered firewood from the forest floor. The only sounds were his labored breathing and the crackle of dry twigs snapping below his feet. He was huffing not from exertion but from irritation.

He shouldn't have lost control like that. It had been sloppy and indulgent, and he prided himself on not making careless mistakes.

Stupid.

He'd risked exposure by walking right through the front door of McCandless' condo building and jimmying her lock. Ransacking the space she shared with her husband had been satisfying. It had enabled him to release the raw, blinding rage that had been building ever since he learned that Anna had named the lawyer as trustee of her estate. He'd enjoyed imagining the shock on their faces when they saw the thorough violation of their home.

But what had he actually accomplished? Not a thing. He hadn't advanced his goals in any way.

It had been a fully wasted day.

He pounded his thigh in frustration. Then he spat in the dirt and wiped his mouth with the back of his hand.

He needed to regroup. Think. Regain control.

He was so close to his goal, and Pulaski had given him the last piece of information he needed. Tomorrow at ten o'clock in the morning, Sasha McCandless was going to walk into the Allegheny County Court of Common Pleas to try to sever his ties with his children. Whether she won or lost, he planned to see to it that the last thing she ever did was walk back out of that courthouse.

He reached into his vest pocket and fished out the satellite phone that the head of Westmoreland County prepper unit had given him with a mixture of pride and embarrassment.

He'd accepted it with gratitude, but he did think it was an extravagant waste. Not for *him;* he needed a secure, untraceable, reliable way to communicate with like-minded men. But he was on the run in an arguably functional society. His situation was different.

What use would anyone possibly have for a satellite phone when the satellites were all knocked out by an apocalyptic weather event or inoperable because the entities that shared the cost of operating them had all collapsed in an economic disaster? A sat-link was no defense against roving bands of desperate, hungry men. Or a man-made plague. Or terrorists who'd seized control of the government.

No matter. Right now, the lack of forethought and good planning on the part of a group of well-intentioned but misguided Western Pennsylvanian comrades was not his problem.

No, his problem was that right now he was in a holding pattern, unable to take any action to move his plans forward until the next day.

As Anna had always said, he wasn't a man who did well with down time.

His hand hovered over the numbers on the phone trying to decide whether it would be productive to call Pulaski again. To what end, though?

A slow grin crossed his face as a better idea crystallized in his mind.

He punched in an old friend's telephone

number—a friend who prided himself on his ability to procure any weapon, fast, no questions asked.

Twenty minutes and two phone calls later, Bricker was en route to rendezvous with someone named "Slim Jim," who would provide him with a clean firearm to replace the one he'd been forced to abandon when he'd fled the compound in New Mexico.

He had his hunting knife, and his handiwork on Anna had established his ability to improvise. But Bricker was never happier than when he was peering through a rifle scope. Even a hand gun would suffice. He could almost feel the satisfying weight in his hand.

He chuckled to himself. What was that Shakespeare quote? "The first thing we do, let's kill all the lawyers." He wasn't much of a literature lover, and he was sure if Anna were alive, she'd delight in telling him he had the context wrong, but as far as he was concerned, it was sound advice.

He neared the designated drop spot and paused in a clearing in the trees to check his watch. A few minutes early, just as he'd planned.

He scanned the park's small picnic area and saw no evidence of an ambush.

He waited several minutes, willing himself to be patient as his excitement grew.

Finally, at the appointed time, he stepped onto the gravel path and headed toward the wooden structure that housed the restrooms.

As he reached the door, a tall, lanky man stepped out of the men's room.

Bricker's surprise was two-fold. One, Slim Jim hadn't timed the drop so as to avoid an in-person meeting. *Sloppy.* And, two, given the younger generation's penchant for irony, he'd assumed anyone going by the name Slim Jim would be a short, rotund guy.

He averted his eyes and studiously avoided meeting the man's gaze.

Slim Jim did the same.

Bricker pushed open the metal door and entered the bathroom. The smell of overheated cleaning chemicals hit him in the face, but he supposed that out of the possible offensive odors he could have expected, bleach was the best of the bunch.

Let's get on with it.

He scanned the row of stalls for feet. None. To be sure, he kicked in each door in the row, setting off a series of bangs as the doors clanged against the metal partitions separating the stalls, one after another. No one was standing on any of the toilet seats.

Satisfied, he walked over to the metal paper towel dispenser closest to the entrance. As promised, it was empty of paper towels. He banged his fist on the unlocked compartment. It swung open. He reached inside and grabbed the package Slim Jim had left.

The weapon had been wrapped up in several blue, plastic grocery bags emblazoned with the Giant Eagle logo and held shut with masking tape. It wasn't particularly elegant, but it had gotten the job done.

He ripped open the bags and tossed them in the trash then took a few seconds to briefly examine the gun before checking the safety on the slide and shoving it into the waistband of his pants. A Beretta Cougar. Compact, concealable, accurate. *Perfect.*

He exited the bathroom. He could detect a bounce in his own step—the result both of his relief at once again being armed and his considerable pride at the efficiency and effectiveness of the larger prepper network. He couldn't claim responsibility for all of its successes, of course. But he knew that he, and men like him, had created the foundation for the organization. And he was rightfully proud.

He caught himself whistling as he hurried away from the rest area.

He vaulted over the wall leading to the creek that tracked the highway above and rolled up his pant legs to wade in.

Cool water rushed around his ankles.

He waded back toward the downtown area and his makeshift camp.

29

For all her eye-rolling at Connelly's suggestion that Maisy would act like a stereotypical, scoop-hungry reporter, Sasha wasn't remotely surprised when her friend and neighbor pulled out a notebook the moment she spotted them talking to the patrolman in front of the door to the condo.

She was heartened, however, to see Maisy second-guess her journalistic instinct and stuff the notepad back into her bag before trotting over to join them.

She shot Connelly a look as if to say 'see, she has a soul.'

"Darlin', I'm so sorry about your place. Both of you," she said in her juicy-as-a-peach Southern accent. She swooped in to give Sasha and Connelly each a tight hug.

Maisy was one of those people who hugged like she meant it. She squeezed just a little more warmly and just a touch longer than most people. As a result, Sasha found her hugs to be almost maternal in their comfort. She filed that thought away under 'things to remember if you adopt a half-dozen children: give good hugs.'

She laughed aloud at herself.

Maisy, Connelly, and the baby-faced police officer all eyed her with varying degrees of concern.

"Sorry," she muttered.

"You're prolly in shock," Maisy proclaimed.

She feinted for the notepad again, and Connelly headed her off.

"You're right. She probably is. We can't thank you enough for noticing the break in and securing the condo until the police arrived, but you don't have to stick around. I know you have plans this afternoon," he said in a sincere tone.

"Don't be silly. I called that boy and told him we could have our lunch date some other time. My girlfriend needs me, don't you, sweet sugar?"

Maisy turned her brilliant eyes on Sasha.

"Honestly, I'll be fine. I'm sure we'll have lots of

boring questions to go over with the police and my insurance agent. You go on and do something fun —hit a sale at Banana Republic. I'll catch up with you later," Sasha promised.

Maisy drooped visibly.

The uniformed officer shuffled his feet. Sasha could see the wheels turning as he searched for a legitimate-sounding reason to keep Pittsburgh's most attractive news personality on the scene just a little bit longer.

Sasha looked more closely at him. Dark, closed-cropped hair, dark eyes, full lips. He was definitely Maisy's type, if a touch on the young side.

"Actually, why don't you see if Officer …."

"Tryorus, Ma'am. Dan Tryorus."

"Officer Tryorus can give you an official statement while Connelly and I poke around inside. Maybe you could file a short piece? I mean, if it's a slow news day. I doubt a routine break-in in Shadyside will merit coverage."

Maisy brightened.

Officer Tryorus was torn between performing his duties and flirting with the bombshell who was gazing up at him expectantly. "Well, uh, actually, I wouldn't call it a routine kind of situation. But it might be a good idea if you and Agent—uh, Mr., uh, Agent—Connelly took a look around and let me know if anything seems to be missing. I'll stay posted right here at the door."

Connelly suppressed a grin at the police officer's blatant excuse to hang around with Maisy, as well as his awkward manner of address. Clearly, Maisy had already filled in the young officer as to his law enforcement background. Lord knew what she'd told him about Sasha.

He started through the door then stopped short. "You've confirmed the premises are vacant, right?"

Officer Tryorus dragged his eyes away from Maisy long enough to snap to attention and answer.

"Yes, sir!" he barked. "I personally checked in every closet and under every piece of furniture. The perpetrator's long gone and the scene is secure, sir."

"Thank you, officer."

Connelly rested a feather light hand on Sasha's back and gently guided her into the condo.

She was glad for his touch because when she saw the destruction of their home she stumbled backward, and he was there to catch her.

The thoroughness of the mayhem took her breath away for a moment.

Every chair was upturned, the leather sliced open. Smashed picture frames were piled atop leather-bound legal books, their onionskin pages torn out and scattered across the floor.

In the kitchen, the cabinets hung open. Glasses had been swept off the shelves and gone crashing onto the tile, where slivers of various sizes glinted in the light. The colorful ceramic dishes they'd brought back from their honeymoon in Costa Rica had been tossed onto the heap. Shards of the festive indigenous pottery stuck out from the debris at menacing angles. A row of coffee mugs that had been hanging on hooks over the sink had been scattered across the counters.

A sob caught in her throat. Connelly rubbed her back.

"The noise must have been spectacular," she managed.

"I'll bet. It's lucky Java was at the house with the Bennetts," he observed.

It was a blessing. A terrified house cat cowering in a corner would only have made the scene more painful.

"We're never going to be able to tell if anything's missing."

"Nothing's missing," Connelly told her.

"How can you be so sure? Look at this mess."

"Exactly. Look at this mess. This isn't the handiwork of someone who was methodically looking for something. Someone—and let's not pretend we don't know who it was—did this in a rage."

She knew he was right.

The desecration was too absolute, too personal to be anything other than a message from Jeffrey Bricker.

"Let's go look at the bedroom," she said.

Her throat was dry and tight, and it burned when she spoke. Her voice sounded strangled to her ears.

Connelly grabbed her hand, interweaving his fingers through hers, as they mounted the stairs to the loft bedroom, the space where they shared their most intimate moments.

If anything, the mess was worse up there.

Their comforter was shredded into long strips. Down covered the room as if there'd been an indoor snowstorm. The wrought iron candle holder that had hung on the wall above the headboard was bent into a twisted mass in the corner of the room, its votive holders scattered in every direction. The heavy silk bedclothes were hacked into pieces and tossed in a pile.

A quick peek into the bathroom confirmed more of the same.

Smashed glass bottles of perfume joined overturned shampoo and body wash bottles on the floor, their contents poured out and mixed together in an eye-wateringly fragrant slick of liquid. Towels formed misshaped mounds in every corner of the bathroom. Pain relievers and allergy medications rolled underfoot like miniature marbles.

But it was the sight of her master closet that forced her to finally release the tears she'd been fighting back.

It wasn't the fact that her entire wardrobe of suits, jackets, sweaters, and dresses was slashed and ruined, hanging haphazardly from hangers or thrown on the ground, that broke her down so much as the intimacy of the attack on the items she'd worn. Almost as if he'd imagined her skin as he'd stabbed, cut, and hacked his way through her closet.

Connelly's clothes were in the same condition, his neat rows of color-coordinated shirts and ties strewn across the floor, ripped and ruined.

"Hey," he said with obviously forced joviality, "I guess it's a good thing you dragged along seventy-million pairs of shoes with you after all."

She faked a laugh even though she could tell he was as worried and angry as she was.

His olive skin had paled almost to white, and

he was doing that tense, jaw-clenching thing he did.

"Why did he do this?" she whispered, asking the question more to herself than to Connelly.

But he looked up from the pinstriped suit he was trying to salvage and locked eyes with her.

"He wanted to do two things: send us a message and vent his rage," he said analytically.

"Well message received. What rage specifically are you talking about, Mr. Special Agent? I can tell you have a theory, Connelly. When are you going to realize I can read you just as well as you read me, hmm?"

The tension around his eyes melted, and he managed a brief grin. But it didn't last long.

"The personal nature of the vandalism, the invasion of our space, the viciousness of the destruction—they're all indications that he's reacting to what he perceives as *our* invasion of *his* personal space. He wants us out of his kids' lives."

She nodded. "But he's getting sloppy. What's the term—decompensating?"

Connelly's face was grim.

"He may be. Bricker's hallmarks have always been organization, control, and precision. Even the violence of the attack on Allison isn't completely out of character. But, this … this is uncharacteristic."

Sasha's pulse raced just under her skin, so fast that she felt faint. If Bricker was falling apart, what would that mean for the kids?

30

Friday

Sasha twisted the wedding band around on her finger, while she waited for the coffee to brew. In the predawn gloom, she could just make out the thin ring of metal. She replayed the words Connelly had spoken before slipping it onto her finger.

Were they partners—in good times, in bad, for better or worse—or not?

Of course they were, she chided herself. But what did that mean now, in practice, in light of what he'd asked to consider?

Java slunk into the room, creeping low on his belly, as if he could sense her tension. He wrapped himself around her ankles.

She knelt to pet him. As she scratched the spot between his ears, the image of her engagement ring, hanging by a ribbon around his neck, popped into her mind.

Darn you, Connelly.

Of course she wanted children. Maybe. But six of them? At once?

The coffee maker beeped. She stood and filled her oversized mug. She inhaled the deep, satisfying scent of fresh coffee, hot and strong, and took a long swallow.

Her tired eyes burned from lack of sleep.

Java mewled and turned to face the door, his tail swishing expectantly.

A moment later, Sasha heard footsteps in the hallway.

She rested her mug on the counter and waited.

Connelly padded into the room, barefoot and shirtless, wearing nothing but his blue and white striped pajama bottoms.

The side of his face was lined with a red pillow crease. He blinked in the dim light.

"There you are. It's not even five o'clock," he yawned.

"Yeah, I couldn't sleep."

"Are you worrying about the hearing tomorrow?"

"No."

"Thinking about the damage at the condo?"

"No."

She fixed her eyes on his.

He waited.

The room was so quiet she could hear the soft tick of his wristwatch.

Finally she found her voice.

"I've been thinking about what you said. About kids."

He reached for a coffee mug and filled it before responding.

"You mean about adopting the Bennetts?"

"Yes."

He looked at her closely. "That's a big decision."

She arched a brow at the obvious statement. "You think?"

A slow smile spread across his mouth. "Yeah, kinda. So what are you thinking?"

"I don't know what I'm thinking. I mean, six kids?"

"They're great kids."

"Connelly. There are six of them."

His gray eyes grew serious. "I know, Sasha. And they're unlikely to get to stay together if they enter the system. Imagine losing your mother, effectively losing your father, and having what's left of your family split up like a litter of puppies."

She could feel tears building behind her own tired eyes.

"I know."

"Well?"

She looked at her husband for a long time, for what felt like days.

She had the hard-won ability to will herself not to cry—a skill she'd learned as the youngest of four children and the only girl. For once, she didn't employ it.

She leaned her head against Connelly's chest and let her hot tears fall. She was scared, and confused, and worried.

Finally she whispered, "I don't know."

He smoothed her hair with his warm, strong hand. She listened to the steady beat of his heart under her cheek.

"You don't have to know now. Just give it time and the answer will come," he whispered back.

She closed her eyes and nodded, but she didn't understand how he could be so sure.

"Sasha?"

"I heard you. I'm trying."

He tipped her chin up and pierced her with his soft gray eyes.

"I know."

Then he covered her lips with a kiss that promised no matter what she decided, he'd be there.

And then someone was tugging on the hem of her shirt.

She wiped her tears from her cheeks and glanced down.

Calla grinned up at her and thrust a brown hairbrush and a ponytail holder into her hands.

"Will you do my hair, please? I want a braid like the princess in *Frozen*."

Sasha exchanged glances with Connelly over the girl's head. His puzzled shrug told her that he was as clueless about Disney princess hairstyles as she was.

"Um, sure."

She took Calla's small, warm hand and led her over to the table and chairs in the breakfast nook.

"While you're doing Calla's hair, I'm going to jump in the shower and then make sure Cole and Brianna are awake," Connelly said.

She nodded as he left the room and focused on separating Calla's fine, silky hair into sections.

"Tell me again where you're taking Cole?" the girl asked in her tiny voice.

"Cole is going to come to court with me and

Leo to talk to a judge about some grownup things," she explained. *Over my strenuous objections.*

"Cole's not a grownup."

"That's right. He isn't, is he? But he's *almost* a grownup. And now that your mom is gone, he feels like he should help take care of grownup stuff for your family."

She threaded the sections into a braid, careful not to tug too hard. She could still remember how her head used to smart when Valentina would attack her curls, beating them into submission with a brush and then twisting them into tight pigtails.

"Oh. Because our dad's a bad guy, right?"

Sasha froze with the brush dangling mid-air.

How was she supposed to answer that one?

"Um, your dad did some bad things. Do you remember him?"

"No." Calla's voice was matter of fact.

"Oh."

She resumed braiding.

"Is Naya going to come over and watch us?"

"She has a test today, so Uncle Hank is going to come over instead, okay?"

"Yeah, that's great! He lets us have chocolate cake for breakfast!"

"Wow, that sounds ... sugary."

Calla giggled.

"Are you done? Can I see?"

Sasha twisted the elastic band around the bottom of the braid and stepped back to admire her handiwork.

"Yep, all done."

She picked up the girl and carried her over to the microwave so she could see her reflection. Calla flipped the braid over her shoulder and squealed.

"I look *just* like Elsa! Oh, thank you, thank you! I love you, Sasha!"

She threw both hands around Sasha' neck and squeezed her like only a toddler can.

Sasha rubbed her back.

"You're very welcome, Princess Elsa."

As soon as she returned Calla to the floor, the girl took over running, legs and arms pumping, as she raced to find her siblings and show off her hair.

Sasha picked up her coffee and sipped at it. She was so lost in thought, she didn't really even notice that it was room temperature.

31

Andy knotted his tie and ran a shaking hand over his hair.

Courtroom jitters, he told his reflection.

You're full of crap, he answered himself.

It was true, of course. It had been years since he'd gotten nervous before standing up in a courtroom. Big Gun Pulaski has nerves of steel and balls to match.

But here he was, twenty minutes until show time, hiding in a musty courthouse bathroom trying to get a grip.

He checked his watch. Twenty minutes until show time.

Acid swirled in his stomach. He hadn't eaten a meal or caught more than a cat nap since receiving the call from Bricker on Wednesday. He was agitated and shaky from lack of food and sleep. And fear.

Bricker had promised he'd be well-compensated if he performed well.

But Andy had latched on to what his client had left unsaid. What would Bricker do to him if he didn't shine? What if the judge appointed McCandless despite his objections? Would Bricker kill him?

Get. A. Grip.

He washed his hands and lobbed the paper towel toward the trashcan.

If it goes in, it's a sign that you're gonna win.

The crumpled towel bounced off the rim of the can and landed on the floor.

Andy closed his eyes for a moment to clear his mind.

He had to stomp out the fear and blaze into Judge Perry-Brown's courtroom, no holds barred, with all the fury he could muster.

His career, and maybe his life, depended on it.

It was time for his pre-game ritual.

He did a quick check of the bathroom to confirm that he was alone. Then he leaned close to the mirror and imagined himself as a blue-faced Mel Gibson in "Braveheart." He took a breath then whispered the lines where William Wallace roused the men before battle. At the end, he threw back his head and roared, "Freedom!"

His voice echoed off the tile floor and walls. His heart thudded in his chest. The Big Gun was ready.

32

Sasha nodded and pretended to listen to whatever last-minute advice Will was hurriedly trying to impart as they walked up the wide white courthouse steps. It didn't matter what he was saying. She already knew how she planned to approach the hearing.

She found that Krav Maga training principles applied almost as well to her trial preparations as to her self-defense routines. Before a court appearance, she rehearsed her planned moves and responses until they became automatic. She didn't have to think about them, which allowed her to free up her mental capacity for identifying and readjusting to unplanned moves that her adversary or the court threw at her.

For her, it worked.

For a belt-and-suspenders guy like Marsh, who memorized a script and refused to deviate from it, her method would have been disastrous. And for an off-the-cuff blusterer who relied on his quick wit and theatrical delivery like her late mentor, Noah, it would have been suffocating. But for her, the structure was freeing. And calming.

In fact, considering she was walking into a courtroom to face off against a truly horrible human being, who was representing an even more disgusting person, in a matter that would decide the course of the lives of six children she cared about, she was calmer than she had any right to be. Placid, even.

A quick glance back at Connelly and Cole as she stepped through the doors into the vestibule sent a wave of worry through all that tranquility, though.

Cole was pale. And sweating.

She put a hand out to stop Will and they moved to the side of the lobby to wait.

Connelly shot her a worried look and jerked his head toward the boy as he stopped next to her.

"Here, can you hold this for me, please?" she asked, handing him her trial bag.

"What? Naya's not here to carry your briefcase, so I have to?" he teased her.

"Something like that."

Cole was staring at the metal detectors with a distant look.

"Are you okay? You don't have to go through with this, you know."

He kept his eyes pinned over her shoulder and gulped.

"I dunno."

She turned toward Connelly.

"Okay, why don't you and Will go ahead. I'll stay here with Cole for a bit and meet you up there."

Connelly glanced from her to Cole then said, "Well at least have him wait on the other side of the security scanners. Just in case."

As in, *just in case his father decides to storm the lobby in a murderous rage.*

"Uh, I need to just sit down for a minute," Cole mumbled.

He half-stumbled toward the nearest bench, but Connelly shook his head.

"Not here. Sasha, since I'm apparently sneaking your knife through security, can you and Will lend Cole a hand?"

Connelly shook his head at her attempt to con him and walked over to a bored-looking police officer gabbing with the scanner operator.

She felt the questions in Will's eyes about the knife comment and a blush crept up her neck.

She cleared her throat and focused on Cole.

"What's he doing?" Cole croaked, nodding toward Connelly.

"He's flexing his federal agent muscle to avoid going through the metal detector with his gun."

"Oh."

Cole's entire body seemed to relax in response to the news that Connelly was armed. He let her guide him toward the little cluster formed by Will, Connelly, and the cop.

Their heads were bent over some official-looking document that Connelly had pulled from his breast pocket.

The police officer was nodding with enthusiasm and self-importance. Based on the officer's conduct, she suspected Connelly had managed to convince him that something critical to national security was about to go down in the Allegheny County Courthouse.

She hid her smile and placed a hand on Connelly's arm.

"Are we good here?" she asked.

The police officer snapped his eyes to her.

"Is this the attorney and client, sir?" he asked Connelly.

“Affirmative,” Connelly answered in his best law enforcement voice.

Behind her, she heard Cole coughing into his hand.

“You’re all cleared, ma’am. Your party can circumvent the scanner and just shoot up that staircase to your right.”

“Thank you, officer,” Will interjected, eager to be on his way. “Let’s go.”

Connelly handed over her trial bag with a knowing smirk.

Will took off for the stairs at a brisk pace, and she had to trot to keep up with him.

Connelly and Cole trailed behind. Connelly refolded his paper and returned it to his pocket. Cole took a final backward glance at the lobby area and exhaled. The color was already returning to his face.

33

Sasha scanned the rows of seats as they entered Judge Perry-Brown's courtroom. A cadre of senior citizens had already claimed the back row and were settled in. In the middle of the room, two brightly-scrubbed law students sat side-by-side in their brand-new suits, legal pads and pens out and ready on their laps. Interns, no doubt. And way over in the far corner, partially obscured by a wall that jutted out, was an unkempt middle-aged man.

Sasha squinted, trying to determine if he was the same guy from last time.

She didn't realize she'd stopped mid-aisle until Connelly bumped into her back.

"Sorry."

"It's my fault," she whispered over her shoulder.

"Is everything okay?"

"Not sure."

She took a second look at the man, trying to search his face, but he had his head turned to the wall. He seemed to be avoiding her gaze.

She continued on to the counsel table and dumped her bag beside Will, who was already seated and looking at her with a concerned expression.

She flashed him a reassuring smile then strolled over to the bar separating the gallery from the well and gestured for Connelly and Cole to meet her there.

They had just settled into the front row, but they hurried over to see what she wanted.

Connelly leaned over the railing.

"What's up?"

She directed her comments to Cole. "Don't look, but there's a guy sitting in the far corner, way in the back. He's wearing a green Army jacket. After you sit back down, wait a minute or two and then casually glance over and see if you recognize him as one of your father's followers."

She forced herself not to look in the man's direction and to keep her tone unconcerned, but worry flashed in Connelly's eyes. He patted his jacket, where she knew his Glock was holstered.

Cole gnawed on his lower lip.

"Here? You think my dad has a plant here?"

She reached over the bar and patted down his cowlick. His hair popped right back up.

"Probably not. He's probably just some down-on-his-luck guy enjoying the air conditioning. But just in case, do me a favor and take a peek, okay?"

She smiled broadly at him.

The door swung open, and Pulaski entered the courtroom.

She kept the smile pasted firmly in place and walked back to counsel's table.

As Pulaski claimed the seat next to hers, she twisted her neck and caught Cole's eye.

He shook his head no. He didn't recognize the homeless guy.

Connelly's tense face relaxed a fraction.

Sasha exhaled in relief.

"Breathless already, McCandless?" Pulaski cracked.

She turned to him. "You're looking awfully green, Andy. You feeling okay?"

She said it mainly to rattle him, but it was true. He looked sickly. And scared.

For a fleeting moment, something like

sympathy swelled in her—after all, he hadn't chosen to represent a sociopathic criminal.

Then he winked at her and licked his lips, and any kind feelings evaporated.

"Just gearing up to take you down. It's gonna be the highlight of my career." He bared his teeth in an approximation of a smile.

Will stiffened and shifted in his chair.

She turned away from Pulaski and caught Will's attention.

"What a putz," she said loudly enough for Pulaski to hear.

Will searched her face.

"Are you ready?"

"Ready as I'll ever be."

She removed a legal pad from her briefcase, taking care not to disturb the knife nestled in the bottom of the bag.

Bev, the judge's clerk, looked up from her paperwork and checked the time. Then she picked up the telephone to her right and murmured into the receiver.

Sasha knew she was telling the judge that all parties were present and ready to go.

Showtime.

The doors leading from the judge's chambers opened, and she entered the courtroom with her large handbag dangling over the crook of her elbow.

Sasha immediately thought of Madeleine Albright, who had an assistant whose job was to carry her purse. If she were a judge, she'd at least press a law clerk into service. It didn't seem very judicial to be weighted down with a Coach bag, she mused as she stood to greet the judge.

"All rise. The Honorable Merry Perry-Brown presiding," Bev intoned.

Sasha heard the shuffle of feet and the rustle of fabrics, as Connelly, Cole, and the assorted onlookers got to their feet.

She wondered for an instant if there would be an outburst from the gallery, but no one spoke.

Judge Perry-Brown deposited her purse on the bench and smiled down at the counsel table.

"Good morning, counselors."

"Good morning, Your Honor," they parroted in unison.

They waited until she was situated then folded themselves back into their seats.

The judge scanned the audience, and her eyes settled first on Connelly and Cole. They stood out by virtue of sitting in the front row and because they were both wearing somber dark suits—Cole's was brand new. Sasha had snipped the label off the sleeve just that morning.

"Good morning," the judge said to Cole and Connelly. The curiosity in her voice was bare.

"Good morning, Your Honor," Connelly replied.

He nudged Cole.

"Good morning, Your Honor," the boy mumbled.

"And you are?"

"Agent Leo Connelly, Your Honor," Connelly said.

Sasha suppressed the urge to turn around and ask him what precisely he was an agent of these days. Agent of change?

The judge arched a shaped brow and waited for further elucidation.

"I'm Cole Bennett, Your Honor," Cole finally said in a halting, strangled voice.

Will coughed discreetly. "Mr. Connelly and the young man are with us."

Recognition lit in the judge's eyes.

"Mr. Pulaski, Ms. McCandless, and Mr. Volmer—in my chambers. Now. You, too, Mr. Agent Man. Bring the boy."

She grabbed her purse and flounced back to her chambers.

Pulaski was muttering under his breath while he gathered up his papers.

Sasha tossed her notepad in her bag and snapped it closed.

"You folks ready?" Bev asked, pausing in the middle of the well.

"Yes, ma'am," Will chirped.

"Well, follow me, then."

She held open the small gate cut into the bar and let the attorneys pass.

Connelly and Cole met them in the aisle.

"What's going on?" Connelly whispered in her ear. His breath tickled her hair.

She just shrugged. If Connelly understood nothing else about the American justice system, he should know by now that judges could be as mercurial and unpredictable as any self-respecting three year old.

They tromped down the aisle behind the judge's clerk.

As they neared the door, the man in the Army jacket tracked them with his hooded eyes.

34

Pat half-jogged through the alley. He skidded to a stop in front of Bricker and braced his hands on his knees to catch his breath.

Bricker jumped to his feet.

"What happened?"

Even though he hadn't been running particularly hard, the homeless man put up a hand and wheezed, red-faced.

"Chambers," he panted.

Bricker balled his hands into fists and forced himself to wait while Pat caught his breath.

"The judge brought all the lawyers back into her chambers. The agent and the kid, too."

"Kid?"

Pat nodded. He got his breathing back under

control and said, "Along with the same lawyers from last time, some serious-looking guy—said his name was Agent Connelly—and a teenaged boy were there. Cole Bennett, that was the kid's name. They came in with the lady lawyer. I don't know what the relationship between Connelly and the kid is. They seemed tight."

Leo Connelly and Clay? Anger boiled in Bricker's gut.

Stay in control. Don't explode.

He tamped down the hot rage and said, "Go on."

Pat gave him a questioning look. "You okay, man? You're sweating."

"I'm fine," he said between clenched teeth. "Get on with your story."

"Uh, sure. So, I don't know how long they'll be back there. I asked some of the old farts—they're regulars. They said usually a judge has a private conference back in chambers and deals with whatever the confidential things are and then they all come back out into the courtroom. But not always. They all stuck around, so they must think she's going to do something in the courtroom. I thought I should let you know, though."

"You did the right thing."

Pat stared at him.

"What?" Bricker hissed.

"What should I do now?"

"What do you mean, what should you do? Get your ass back in there!"

Pat snapped to attention instantly.

Bricker wondered if he was a combat veteran.

"Yes, sir!"

He turned around and hauled himself back toward the court.

Bricker hoped the man didn't drop dead from exertion. At least not until he reported back on what the devil McCandless was up to and why she'd brought his eldest son into court.

Now he wished he'd risked creeping closer to the front of the building to see them arrive. At the time, he'd decided to hunker down in the alley so as not to tip off McCandless or whichever of her pathetic male lackeys were tagging along with her.

But he would have liked to have laid eyes on Clay once more, even from a distance.

He slumped back against the wall and resumed his seated position, resting his head against the cool bricks as if he were just another hungover vagrant dozing in an alley.

But his mind raced as he imagined Clay lapping up Connelly's pro-government propaganda.

No. Not Clay.

But the words rang hollow. Clay had deserted him—and the cause—at the compound. He'd piled the younger kids in the car and had fled. Like a coward.

Bricker reached inside his jacket and stroked the Beretta.

During his trial, the story had emerged that Connelly and McCandless had been instrumental in helping his children leave the compound.

He'd never properly conveyed his feelings about that fact.

Today was his chance.

Keep a lid on your temper and wait for your shot.

35

Judge Perry-Brown unzipped her robe and stepped out of it. Then she tossed it over the back of her leather chair and lowered herself into the seat.

She waved her hand in the direction of her three guest chairs. As if by unspoken agreement, Connelly and Will stepped back and leaned against the wall, leaving the chairs for the others.

Pulaski claimed the one closest to the judge's desk. Sasha took the one furthest from Pulaski and tried not to stare at the judge's attire.

In her experience, most judges—male or female—wore business attire under their robes. Not Judge Perry-Brown. She was wearing a light red t-shirt that made Connelly's rattiest shirt look like high fashion. It was worn paper thin, almost bare in spots, which was hardly surprising considering that the faded black letters proclaimed the wearer a member of the "Upper Saint Clair High School Swim Team 1974." The judge's t-shirt was literally older than Sasha.

Once Cole was settled into the chair between Sasha and Pulaksi, the judge leaned forward and rested her tanned forearms on her desk.

"Okay, people, we're going to do this without a court reporter. So I'm telling you upfront, Mr. Pulaski—anything we discuss in here and any decisions I make will be considered off the record and unappealable. Got it?"

Pulaski arranged his face into a hurt expression.

"Yes, ma'am. But is there some reason that comment is directed solely to me, Your Honor?"

The judge twisted her mouth into a dour expression.

"Come on, Andy. Do you really need me to answer that?"

He didn't respond immediately, so she continued, "I don't know Ms. McCandless or Mr. Volmer personally, but I do know that *their* reputations don't precede them. You've earned a short leash. They haven't."

Pulaski's face darkened, but he held his tongue.

"Moving on. I have to say I'm not sure what to do about maintaining the secrecy of your client's identity, Ms. McCandless and Mr. Volmer. The courts are open for a reason. That said, if you want to make a compelling argument for closing this proceeding, I'm all ears."

Sasha and Will exchanged a look.

They'd anticipated this issue and had spent a considerable amount of time hashing out a response that they, Hank, and the Bennett kids could live with.

Will nodded to indicate that Sasha should take the lead.

"Well, Your Honor, to be perfectly frank, the Department of Justice doesn't share your concerns, or ours. They've terminated the Bennett children from the witness protection program."

"What?!"

The judge exploded out of her chair like a firecracker.

"Justice and Homeland Security are taking the position that Alison Bennett was the protected witness, not the children. She's gone. So they're out." Sasha didn't sugarcoat the facts.

Judge Perry-Brown wheeled around to face Connelly.

"Agent Connelly, tell me your wife's mistaken."

Sasha wrinkled her brow. *How did the judge know they were married?*

Connelly nodded solemnly. "I wish I could, Judge."

The judge huffed. "So now what?"

"The Bennett children don't want to remain in hiding, Your Honor. The older kids have discussed it amongst themselves. What they hope happens is that this court terminates Jeffrey Bricker's paternal rights and allows them to continue to live under their new identities but not under the strictures of the witness protection program, obviously. So they have no objection to the hearing going forward in open court."

The judge turned and blinked, owl-eyed, at Cole.

"Is that accurate, son?"

"Yes, ma'am."

There was a long pause. The judge appeared to be weighing her options.

Pulaski cleared his throat.

"If I may, Your Honor. I have some information that may clarify your path forward."

"What's that, Counselor?"

"I received a telephone call from my client a few days ago. He doesn't want to contest the termination of his parental rights."

Sasha felt her mouth hanging open and clamped her jaw closed.

"I beg your pardon, Andrew?" The judge turned to Pulaski, confusion painted across her face.

Pulaski shrugged.

"That's what he said."

Cole was the one who had the presence of mind to ask the obvious question. "What's the catch?"

"He does object to Attorney McCandless serving as trustee of the irrevocable trust."

"What?" Will sputtered. "If he's giving up his parental rights, how does he even have standing to object to anything related to the trust?"

Pulaski shrugged again and spread his hands wide. "How should I know? Do I look like an estates and trusts lawyer?"

The question may have been hypothetical, but the answer was no. Marsh Alverson was the quintessential estates and trusts lawyer. And Pulaski and Marsh didn't look to be of the same species, let alone the same profession. But the judge didn't let that distract her.

"You're a member of the bar, Andrew. And you're advancing a position. So argue it."

Panic flashed in Pulaski's eyes.

"I can't, Your Honor. I'm out of my depth here. And, frankly, I'm going to need some time to prepare."

"Nice try. I'm not granting you any time to do anything. We're marching back out there, and I'm disposing of the parental rights issue. Then you all are going right back on Judge Kumpar's docket. You're his problem from here on out; not mine."

The judge walked over to Cole and crouched in front of his chair.

"Now if I terminate your father's parental rights, you and your siblings are well and truly on your own. You're too young to take on the responsibility for your own care, let alone theirs. Is there anyone—a relative, a friend, anyone—who can take you all in, at least temporarily?"

Cole blinked furiously but didn't speak.

"Son?" the judge prodded him.

Sasha knew he was worrying that the judge would send them all into the foster care system. She shared his fear.

"No," he finally mumbled.

"Judge Perry-Brown," Connelly said, "we've been staying with the kids. We're happy to continue to do so as long as it takes to sort this out."

The judge shot Sasha and Connelly an unreadable look.

After a moment's silence, she said, "Is that okay with you, Cole?"

"Yes, ma'am."

Gratitude flooded the boy's face. Sasha thought she saw tears welling in his eyes. She held her breath and waited for the judge to speak.

"That settles it, then," the judge said.

JUDGE PERRY-BROWN GAVE SASHA, Will, and Pulaski just enough time to reassemble at their table before she swept into the courtroom and resumed the session.

Everyone bobbed up, and she instructed them to sit.

Once the court reporter indicated that she was ready to start recording the session, the judge squared her shoulders and locked eyes with Cole.

"After a session in chambers, the parties have resolved the outstanding motion to terminate parental rights as follows: Mr. Bricker's counsel represents that his client does not contest the termination of his parental rights with regard to the six minor Bennett children. Accordingly, it is so ordered that, effective immediately, Mr. Bricker's parental rights are hereby terminated. The effect, if any, of said termination on the disposition of the estate of Allison Bennett is reserved for determination by the probate court. Finally, this Court finds that the minor Bennett children are currently being adequately cared for by Attorney McCandless and Mr. Connelly and finds that arrangement is not to be disturbed, either by Children and Youth Services or any other entity. I've contacted Judge Kumpar's chambers and advised him of the time-sensitive nature of this matter. His deputy assures me that Ms. Bennett's probate will be expedited."

The judge paused and looked down at the court reporter.

"Off the record."

The woman's fingers paused mid-air.

"Ms. McCandless, Mr. Volmer, this Court thanks you for your service. Mr. Bennett, I wish you and your siblings the very best. Mr. Connelly and Ms. McCandless, as the mother of two grown sons, the Court wishes you much luck." The judge's smile faded. "Mr. Pulaski, submit your paperwork for reimbursement through the clerk's office."

Will pumped his fist in silent victory. Sasha

knew how he felt. The judge's stilted words had sent a thrill of excitement through her.

A glance to her left revealed that they sent something more akin to a wave of revulsion through Pulaski, but seeing as how he was so revolting to the rest of the world, she figured that was just karma catching up to the Big Gun.

She twisted in her seat and caught Connelly's eye. He was grinning—a giant smile that stretched across his face and made his eyes all squinty and crinkly. Beside him, Cole wore an equally goofy smile. As soon as he noticed her looking at him, Cole yawned as if he were bored. She threw him a wink.

The rest of the gallery seemed to be completely unaffected by the decision. They just shifted in their seats and waited for Bev to call the next case. All except the Army jacket man—he was already bolting through the door to the hallway.

36

Sasha led the small group down the stairs, their excited chatter combining with the clatter of their footsteps to create an echoing din.

Even in the afterglow of the judge's decision, caution was foremost in their mind.

"I'll go get the car and bring it around. You wait here," Will offered as soon as they emerged from the stairwell into the worn lobby, with all its faded glamour.

"I'll come with you," Connelly said in a tone that didn't invite disagreement.

The last thing they needed was for Bricker to overpower Will and use him as leverage.

Connelly gave a half-salute to his new friend at the scanner and hurried off with Will.

"Let's wait over here," Sasha suggested to Cole, guiding him to a bench on the protected side of the security line.

They settled themselves on the bench and sat in silence.

After a moment, she asked, "How's it feel?"

He snapped his head toward hers. "Having no dad, you mean?"

"Yeah."

He considered the question.

"Good, mostly."

"I bet, though, there's some sadness, too, that it had to be this way, right?"

She wasn't really sure how to encourage a teenage boy to share his emotions. She felt self-conscious and awkward.

He gave her a long, unreadable look. Finally, he shrugged.

"I dunno."

The old-fashioned elevator directly across the way dinged and the doors parted. The small crowd waiting to ascend to the courtrooms on the floors above and have justice dispensed, denied, or more likely delayed, stepped back to let the passengers exit..

The first person off the elevator was the guy in the army jacket. He pushed aside a slow-moving older man and hurried toward the front of the building.

A warning pricked at the base of Sasha's skull. Her gut told her to follow the man.

But she had to stay with Cole. This was no time to take unnecessary risks.

A buzz of adrenaline shot through her system, and the skin on her arms pimpled into goosebumps.

She glanced at Cole.

"Listen. Don't move until Leo and Will show up. I'll be right back, but if they get here before me, just tell them I had to take care of something."

"Where are you going?"

"Nowhere. Just promise me you'll stay right here."

"Sure."

She craned her neck. The guy was almost to the doors. She couldn't sit here and impress upon Cole how serious she was. She'd miss her chance.

"I'll be right back," she said over her shoulder as she started weaving through the crowd of jurors and court personnel returning from lunch.

She skirted a woman pushing a double stroller then broke into a jog. The man in the Army jacket pushed through the revolving door that would spit him out on Grant Street.

She gripped her trial bag against her body and followed him out of the building and down the stairs to the sidewalk. Just before he reached the corner, he made a sudden right and turned into a narrow alley.

She desperately wanted to stop and take out the knife, but she didn't dare—she was more afraid of losing him than of wandering into a dark alley without a readily accessible weapon.

Her heart thrummed in her throat as she stepped into the alley.

He was walking briskly—like a man with a purpose.

She hesitated. If she followed too closely her heels clacking against the bricked-over ground would give her away.

As she was trying to convince herself to move forward, the man looked over his shoulder, as if he'd heard her.

She shrank back along the wall of the nearest building, flattening herself against the surface and trying not to think about how dirty her cream-colored jacket had to be getting.

He froze for a moment, then turned back and continued along the alley. Just past a row of dumpsters, he stopped and stepped into a nook between two structures.

She hoped he hadn't just gone through a passageway out of the alley. Slowly, silently, she removed her cell phone and the knife from her bag. Then she reclosed the bag and gently set it on the ground. She crept closer to the niche the man had disappeared into.

I sure hope this isn't an ambush, she caught herself thinking. Mainly because Daniel would be bitterly disappointed if his star student had allowed herself to be lured into a trap. She'd *never* hear the end of it.

"The judge terminated the father's rights." A gravelly voice rumbled from within the space.

"Any other rulings?" A second voice asked.

She peeked around the corner of the building. The man from the courtroom was standing in front of another man who sat sprawled against a wall. The seated man rose to standing. Her heart seemed to stop for a moment and a chill ran down her spine.

It was Jeffrey Bricker, no question about it. The silver hair, buzz-cut close to his scalp. The military bearing.

She pulled back around the corner and listened hard.

"Uh, I didn't get the details because they were in her office for part of this, but it sounded like the attorney representing the Bricker guy asked her not to approve the woman lawyer as trustee of some trust."

"What did the judge say to that?"

"She said it wasn't her decision to make. She was sending them back to the first judge, the one from the other day, to decide."

"Now?"

"No, but she said soon."

"What else happened?"

"Oh, right, the boy and his brothers and sisters are going to stay with the lawyer and her husband until—"

"What?" Bricker's rage echoed off the bricks.

Sasha fumbled with her phone and pulled up her contacts list. She keyed out a message to Connelly and Hank:

BRICKER's in the alley between Grant and Ross. Hurry.

NOW WHAT? She couldn't very well call 9-1-1, unless she wanted to reveal herself. But there was no way Bricker was walking out of this alley without handcuffs and leg chains. Not if she had anything to do with it.

She slipped the phone into the pocket of her suit jacket. Then she shifted the knife from one hand to the other, shaking out her free hands as she did so—first the left, then the right. Her mind raced.

She had to hold Bricker here until Connelly showed up. He couldn't slip out of their grasp.

The homeless man stammered, "That's what the judge said."

"Son of a ... what did Pulaski have to say to that? Did that worthless piece of dirt even object?"

"Um, maybe back in the judge's chambers—"

"No. Is that what you're saying, Pat? No, he didn't?" Bricker's voice took on a sharp, chilling quality.

"I don't know," the man hurried to clarify. "I'm sorry."

"I'll kill him."

Bricker delivered the threat in an emotionless, almost clinical, way, but it was anything but empty.

Pat didn't respond, and, from her hiding spot, she couldn't see what the two men were doing. What if Bricker hurt Pat? Even worse, what if he fled?

Stay put. Wait for Connelly.

Her brain was screaming silent orders.

But her hand tightened around the hilt of the

knife and her legs were moving without permission from her cerebral cortex.

She stepped into the opening and blocked the only means of egress.

At the sound of her heels striking the bricks underfoot, both Bricker and Pat turned to stare. The homeless man blinked furiously, as if she were a hallucination that he could clear from his eyes if he tried hard enough. Bricker's eyes widened in surprise, but he quickly flattened his expression into a mask of pure anger.

He looked older, harder, and less polished. His stint in prison and the months of living on the run had etched new lines in his face since she'd seen him last. His eyes were unchanged, though. Icy blue pebbles.

They stared at each other unspeaking, then his eyes drifted to the knife by her side.

"You actually brought a knife to a gun fight. It would be funny, if it weren't so tragic," he commented, gesturing toward his jacket. He reached inside for his handgun.

She ignored the jab and calculated the distance between them. Call it twelve, twelve-and-a-half feet.

Got him. Assuming Daniel was right and she was

fast enough, she could take Bricker down before he got one good shot off. Time to move.

She tensed her thigh muscles and prepared to sprint forward. Then she heard the loud clomp of footsteps in the alley behind her.

Bricker shifted his eyes from her face to a point over her left shoulder.

He raised the gun and leveled it, not at Sasha, but behind her.

"You." The single syllable dripped with disgust.

She risked a quick glance to her rear, expecting to see the welcome sight of Connelly and his Glock. Instead, a panting, wild-eyed Cole stood, feet planted wide, a handgun in his shaking hand aimed at his father.

He stood about twelve feet or so behind her. She was basically situated dead center between the gun-wielding father and son.

Reflexively, she stepped to the side.

"Clay," Bricker breathed.

"The name's Cole," the boy said.

"No, son, your name is Clay Bricker. You can reject me if you want, but there's no denying my blood runs through your veins."

Sasha sucked in her breath. *Where was Connelly already?*

"Why'd you do it?"

"Do what—put your mother down?"

Cole's eyes blazed and he jabbed the gun in the air.

"Why?" he repeated.

"Because she betrayed me, and traitors have to be dealt with as a deterrent. I spared you then, but I won't spare you again, Clay."

"I *told* you. My name is Cole. It'll be pretty funny when I kill you with the gun you got her for protection, don't you think?"

Bricker was laughing.

Sasha's mind raced. She had to stop this, now. It was time to put her head down, run as fast as she could, and aim for his middle. She inhaled, filling her lungs with air, and took off. She sprinted, her arms and legs pumping, her ankles wobbling in the stupid stilettos.

In a flash, she reached him. She didn't hesitate. She wrapped her arms around his midsection, and tackled Cole, pushing him to the ground. She cushioned his fall as much as she could. He blinked away tears and stared up at her in wordless disbelief at her betrayal.

She looked up and saw Bricker advancing on them. He pointed the gun down—toward the ground and their heads. She knew from experience that he wouldn't hesitate to execute someone with a single shot to the head.

She pried Anna's gun out of Cole's hand, swallowed the bile rising in her throat, and aimed the weapon up at Bricker. She stared at his cold eyes and steeled herself. She couldn't believe she was going to have to shoot him. She told herself to squeeze the trigger.

Where the hell was Connelly?

Bricker took aim at the back of Cole's head—

From behind him, Pat swung his own arms wide, knocking Bricker's hand to the side as he fired. The gun bucked, but the bullet arced far to the left and burrowed into the brick wall.

Bricker wheeled around, shouting in incoherent rage, and shoved Pat against the wall.

LEO HAD BEEN RUNNING from the parking garage toward the alley when he heard the unmistakable crack of a gun being fired. From the way it echoed, he knew it had come from within the alley. He poured on the speed, fear of what he might find, pulsing in his mind.

He rounded the corner and assessed the scene in a fraction of a second. Sasha and Cole, cowering on the ground. The homeless man from the courtroom batting at Bricker's arms. Bricker, aiming a gun at Sasha.

Leo reached for his Glock. He squeezed off two steady shots, aimed at Bricker's gun hand. The first whizzed by him. The second grazed Bricker's arm. He lost his footing for a moment, but then he took off running.

Leo stopped and crouched beside Sasha and Cole.

"Are you hurt?" His voice cracked with fear.

"No. We're both fine." She was rocking Cole like an infant. "Go, please. Don't let him get away again."

"No way. I'm not leaving you."

His throat was so tight and dry he could barely force the words out.

"Connelly, please."

"You okay, Cole?" he asked, ignoring the fire in her eyes.

"I would have been if *she* hadn't stopped me," he snarled. He pulled free of Sasha's arms.

Leo and Sasha locked eyes. She shook her head sadly and gestured with the gun.

"He had Allison's gun. He was going to kill his dad."

Jesus. What do you say to that? Leo wondered.

He didn't have to respond because the homeless guy piped up from his spot against the wall. "You hit him. Right bicep."

"Good. Are you okay?"

"Yeah, man. I'm fine." Pat called from his spot against the wall.

Sasha closed her eyes for a moment. When she opened them, tears shimmered, waiting to fall. "I can't believe he's getting away again."

Leo nearly choked on the force of her desperation.

"I'll go after him," he said, even though they both knew Bricker was long gone.

She just nodded.

He holstered his gun and sprinted down the narrow alley.

SASHA WATCHED Connelly disappear from view then turned to Pat.

"Thank you. You saved our lives."

He ducked his head, red-faced. "That guy was Bricker? He killed the kid's mom?"

"Yes."

"I never would have helped him ..." he trailed off, leaving the rest unsaid.

"You didn't know."

He shuffled his feet. "Yeah, I really didn't. Listen, I gotta take off before the cops get here. There might be an old bench warrant for public drunkenness kicking around in the system."

She opened her mouth to argue, to try to convince him to stay, but Cole spoke first.

"Good luck to you, sir."

Pat touched his forehead in a salute and then ambled out of the alley.

Cole glared up at her.

"Why did you stop me?"

"If you shot him, you'd carry guilt with you for the rest of your life."

He shook his head and tried to shove her off, but she held him tight.

"No, I wouldn't. I'd be doing the world a favor. And honoring my mom."

"Look at me." She waited until he met her eyes. "Your mother would *not* want you to 'honor' her in that way. You aren't like him, Cole. You're better than this."

A raw sob broke in his throat and his chest heaved.

"You were going to shoot him," he said.

She blew out a long breath. "That's different. You—we—were in imminent danger." She reached over and smoothed down his sweaty hair.

He jerked away.

"I'm fine," he said stiffly. His cheeks flamed red.

She didn't know what else to say, so she helped him to his feet and they stood in uncomfortable silence waiting for the police to arrive.

37

Leo ran until his throat burned, and then he ran some more. He knew he was on a fool's errand, but he couldn't shake the memory of the resignation in Sasha's eyes. Maybe he'd get lucky and stumble across Bricker.

His heart was still jumping erratically in chest, just as it had been ever since he'd turned the corner into the alley and seen Bricker bearing down on Sasha and Cole with a gun trained on them. He no longer wanted to capture Bricker. He just wanted to kill him.

When he reached the river, he stopped and stared across the water at the still and ghostly steel mills hulking along the opposite bank. Bricker could be anywhere by now—in an abandoned warehouse, under a bridge, on a bus out of town.

He clenched his teeth together to trap the scream of frustration building in his diaphragm.

Now what? Go back to Sasha and tell her he'd failed to protect her once again?

He still woke up most nights, sweating and panicked, dreaming about the aborted raid Bricker had launched against them at their wedding. He needed to put a stop to this. Now.

His cell phone bleated.

He wanted to ignore it, but it was Hank. Hank might have information for him.

"What?" he answered.

"I'm at the scene. I need you to come back."

Two questions fought for primacy. He asked them both. "Why? Where are the kids?"

"Will's with them. He's moved them to Caroline's house for now."

"Jeez, Hank—his secretary? Involve even more civilians, what could go wrong?" he snapped.

There was a long pause.

"I'm going to ignore your tone, Leo. I know you're worried, but you can't afford to get emotional. Now get your ass back here. Your wife has an idea."

"Keep her out of this from here on out, Hank."

Hank's laughter rang in his ear.

"Tell you what, if you think you can sideline

her, be my guest. But, here in reality world, she's the one with the best plan anyone's come up with yet. So if you want to come with us when we use Pulaski as a lure to trap Bricker, you better light a fire under your butt. We're heading out to Monroeville as soon as we work out the details with the locals."

"Hank, no."

"Twenty minutes, Leo. Tick tock."

Hank ended the call.

Leo wasted a few precious seconds cursing his headstrong wife before changing directions and running back toward the city skyline, double time.

"YES, I AM."

"Sasha, no, you're not."

They stared at each other, nostrils flaring, hands on their hips. She had to crane her neck to bore into his eyes with her own, but otherwise they were mirror images. She was sure they looked for all the world like a stereotypical, bickering married couple, but she didn't care. The stakes were too high to care.

"Connelly, we don't have time for this. Hank

said I can come. Detective Markham said I can come. I'm *coming* with you."

Connelly did that twitchy face muscle thing and glared at the local law enforcement representative whom Hank had strong-armed into agreeing to his plan.

Finally, he exhaled shakily. "Fine. But you're wearing a vest."

"Fine, I will. And so will you."

Bulletproof vest? Sure, sign her up. She didn't want to die. She just wanted to be there when they nailed Bricker.

His steely eyes softened.

"Okay. I just—you worried me today in that alley."

He tucked a strand of hair behind her ear.

Her anger melted, replaced by something much gooier.

She smiled but told herself to stay focused.

Pat had confirmed that Bricker had threatened to kill Pulaski just before Sasha revealed herself in the alley. Deprived of his chance to kill her; threatened by his son; and wounded by Connelly, it stood to reason that Bricker would try to soothe his rage with some good, old-fashioned vengeance.

Monroeville's understaffed and overextended municipal police department had agreed to sit on

Pulaski until they got there, but the clock was ticking. The chief had made it clear that he couldn't authorize overtime—not for what amounted to a glorified babysitting job.

Sasha gave Hank a thumb's up signal, and he turned to the detective and started relaying final instructions.

Minutes later, they were in the back seat of a black and white, rumbling over potholes and weaving through Wilkinsburg traffic, speeding toward the William Penn Highway and Pulaski's Miracle Mile strip mall office.

38

Bricker leaned his head back against the greasy bus window and breathed through the pain in his arm. He'd had a narrow escape in the alleyway, and he needed to get someplace where he could rest and recover. Then he'd put a bullet in Pulaski and move on to McCandless and her husband.

As the bus jostled and bumped its way out of the city, his thoughts turned to Clay. A small piece of him was proud that the boy had the stones to confront him. But that sort of paternal sentiment could easily get him killed. The next time he saw Clay, if there was a next time, he'd shoot him as soon as he got the chance.

Right now, though, he had to get to a safe, secluded place. Luckily, he had scouted one days earlier. After he'd called Pulaski on Wednesday, it occurred to him that he needed to get a handle on the lawyer's whereabouts, just in case.

So he'd waited until nightfall and then taken the bus to Monroeville, out to the old Miracle Mile shopping center. From there, he'd circled the area around Pulaski's office, searching for a good location for an ambush.

He'd been surprised to find an excellent spot. It was dark, quiet, and would afford him concealment. The authorities would never think to look for him there.

He had enough water and rations to last forty-eight hours before he had to move on. But he didn't expect he'd need to be there anywhere near that long.

He closed his eyes and conserved his strength for the coming battle.

39

The officer assigned to stay with Pulaski did so until they arrived but not a second longer. As the squad car circled the parking lot and slowed to a stop, the officer inside Pulaski's office was already saying her goodbyes. She was on her way out through the rear door as Sasha, Connelly, and Hank were headed in. They stopped, surrounded by dumpsters, to thank the woman.

"No thanks needed. But that guy's a piece of work. I might just let whoever's after him kill him. No great loss."

She waved a hand back toward the building and laughed.

Sasha suspected the officer's dark humor hinted at her true feelings about Pulaski.

"You know lawyers," she said, giving the woman a sympathetic smile.

She wondered if Pulaski worked at being so unlikeable or if it came naturally.

The officer tipped her cap and continued on her way. Then, she turned back, like she'd just remembered something.

"Your boy got a phone call. Whoever it was scared the crap out of him—he turned pale and started sweating. He blew it off to me like a wrong number, but he went out front and told his secretary to knock off early for the day and then locked the front door."

Hank's eyebrows crawled up his forehead.

"Thanks for letting us know, Officer ..."

"Truman. Like the president. No problem. Good luck."

She reached her car and slid inside, shifted her plastic-covered dry cleaning from the passenger seat to the back, and turned the key in the ignition.

They continued in through the metal loading dock door and ran straight into Pulaski, who was pacing, wild-eyed, in the hallway. When he saw them, he began to rant.

"You're the cavalry? The three of *you*. Fan-freaking-tastic. I might as well swallow a bullet myself and save him the trouble."

Sasha bit her tongue. *Let Hank deal with him.*

"Mr. Pulaski, we believe your client's on his way to kill you. Mr. Connelly and I have a real-time, live link to an elite squad of federal agents that are currently set up in the manager's office in the Applebee's up that hill." Hank pointed toward the back of the building.

Pulaski stopped pacing and listened.

Hank went on, "Mr. Connelly and I are more than competent to save your sorry hide if Bricker shows up." He glanced at Sasha. "As is Ms. McCandless, but I think she'd view your demise as a net benefit to the legal profession."

Sasha coughed to cover her laugh.

"Here's a bullet-proof vest. Put it on." Hank lobbed the heavy vest at Pulaski. "Or don't. I don't really care. I want to catch Bricker. That's my primary goal, just so we're clear."

Pulaski huffed but struggled into the vest.

Then he turned and led them into his office.

"You know, I didn't ask for any of this," he said, stabbing an angry finger toward Sasha. "The judge saddled me with this psychopath."

"Karma," Connelly observed mildly.

Pulaski narrowed his eyes at Connelly but held his tongue.

"Tell us about the phone call," Sasha said.

"What phone call?"

"The phone call that almost made you wet your pants. The one that caused you to send your secretary home and lock the door. You know, the wrong number?" Sasha tried to keep her sarcasm dialed down, but it was a losing battle with this guy.

Pulaski sank into his desk chair and gestured vaguely toward the other two seats. Connelly walked around behind the desk and stared out the window. Hank set up near the door.

"We don't need to sit. We need you to hurry up and start talking, so we can assess the premises and make a plan," Hank told him.

Pulaski's eyes sparked, like he was considering feeding them a lie, but then he shook his head.

"Fine. He called right as I walked back in the door from the hearing. That female cop who just left was standing in the reception area and started yammering about protective duty. Becca butted in and said I had a call I had to take. I took it right there in the lobby. He said he'd heard I didn't contest Sasha's appointment as trustee. I explained that I did but that the judge punted the issue to Kumpar. I *told* him I wasn't a probate lawyer, but he wasn't listening. He just kept saying in this menacing, super-calm voice, 'you're going to pay for this.' So I hung up and sent Becca home."

Pulaski turned and gave Sasha a baleful look. "You can think whatever you want about me, but she's only twenty. She has a kid. I'm not going to let her be exposed out there like a sitting duck."

"What I think is that you might have a heart under your exterior crust of misogynistic crap. But the jury's still out," she told him.

Connelly interjected. "How did he sound?"

"How'd he sound? He sounded crazy, how do you think he sounded?"

"Was he out of breath? Did his voice sound like he was in pain?" Connelly probed, talking slowly as if Pulaski were a child.

"Not really. He just sounded pissed off. Why?"

"Agent Connelly wounded him earlier today, during an altercation outside the courthouse. We don't know his condition, but it's reasonable to assume he's not in peak physical form," Hank said.

"You wounded him? And then you let him get away? For Chrissake."

Connelly's face darkened.

"Listen, Andy, Connolly was more focused on saving Cole's life. If I were you, I'd tread carefully. There's an argument that you exposed Cole by sending that process server around. You don't want to end up in front of the board on an ethics charge, do you?" Sasha smiled sweetly.

Pulaski opened his mouth to fire back.

"Enough," Hank said. "Sasha, stay here with Mr. Pulaski. Leo, come with me. We're going to assess the environment and figure out Bricker's most likely point of entry."

Hank headed for the door. Connelly paused beside Sasha.

"Do you want my gun until we get back?"

"No. I don't trust myself not to shoot him. Besides, I have this." She gestured toward the knife, which was now strapped to her waist.

Connelly smiled and kissed her lightly on the forehead. Then he was gone.

She looked at Pulaski. He looked back at her. Under the best of circumstances, they didn't have a relationship that lent itself to small talk. So they just sat there in silence, watching one another's faces.

40

Bricker focused on keeping his breathing shallow and quiet. Luckily for him, Andy Pulaski kept his office at the temperature of a meat locker, so his noisy air conditioning unit was working hard and loudly.

As an added bonus, the chilled air would help cover any scent he might be giving off, which, to be sure, was probably considerable given that he couldn't remember the last time he showered with the benefit of hot water and indoor plumbing.

He shifted from side to side, trying to keep his muscles loose in the cramped, freestanding wardrobe that was shoved in the corner of Pulaski's office. Despite the cool temperatures, he was soaked in sweat. In part from the stress of having spent the afternoon waiting for a chance to strike.

In part from the hot, searing pain radiating from the bullet wound in his arm.

He'd dug out the bullet with his pocketknife and had done his best to clean it out with the lukewarm water left in his canteen, but eventually he'd need to attend to it better. Antibiotics, a sterile bandage, maybe even some painkillers.

He raised his head and spots danced in front of his eyes in the dim light that managed to penetrate his particle-board hiding spot. His stomach growled.

He had two energy bars stuffed in his pockets, but he didn't dare open them. The rustling of the wrappers would probably go unnoticed by his attorney—for all his blustering and tough guy posturing, Pulaski was a soft target. Unobservant and weak.

But McCandless was just feet away, on the other side of the wardrobe. She was no doubt alert and watchful.

Still, this might be the best chance to strike.

It would take the two feds some time to canvas the space. And if they were thorough, which they surely were, they'd also take the time to walk over to the Vietnamese nail salon on one side of the law office and the computer repair shop on the other, flash their badges, and inspect the shared walls, looking for a crevice, crawlspace, or other means of ingress.

Yes, this was his opening.

Think it through.

Presumably McCandless and Pulaski were both still sitting out there, although if they were, they weren't speaking to each other. He assumed Pulaski would be seated behind his desk, which was directly across from the closet where he hung his cheap suit jackets. There was no telling where McCandless might be, so he had to plan for the worst possibility—act as if she would be standing on the other side of the wardrobe door with a weapon drawn.

His primary goal was to kill Pulaski. Easily achieved. Burst out shooting. He'd almost surely hit him squarely.

But he had secondary and tertiary goals that mattered, too. Secondary goal: kill McCandless. That was nonnegotiable, really. She had to pay, too. But *this* mission was aimed at Pulaski, she was just gravy. Tertiary goal: Avoid capture. It went without saying that he didn't intend to let the government put him back in a cage. But with a squad set up in the restaurant on the hill, according to Richardson, it would be difficult to make a clean escape.

Unless ...

An idea was forming. He probed it for weaknesses, but it seemed solid. Shoot Pulaski and leave him for dead, grab McCandless and use her as a hostage/human shield to make his getaway. Connelly would be paralyzed, unwilling to act to harm her. Richardson would hesitate. And once he was out of the building, the agents rushing to the scene would be instructed to hold their fire. He'd get away and could kill McCandless at his leisure.

As well-thought-out plans went, it stunk. But for an improvised action, it had appeal, logic, and a chance of success.

He fished the chunky Cougar out of his pocket and hefted it in his palm.

One ... two ... go!

He exhaled, kicked the doors open, and leapt from the wardrobe. He wasn't prepared for the light. He squeezed his eyes shut.

Once his vision cleared, he took aim at Pulaski's chest and pumped one, two, three bullets into his mid-section.

Pulaski slumped over his desk.

McCandless had been standing at the window behind the desk. She turned, startled, and then dove for the floor.

Bricker strode toward her.

He could hear footsteps running down the hallway, presumably Connelly and Richardson. But it didn't matter.

He reached down, grabbed a fist full of her hair, and dragged her to her feet. He eyed her chest.

"A bulletproof vest? Nice," he said as he shoved his gun against her temple.

Her eyes were dilated with fear but she kept her breathing under control.

"Thanks. Lucky for Big Gun he's wearing one, too," she said.

He kept the gun snug by her ear while he turned to check on Pulaski.

Crap. It was true. He'd clearly had the wind knocked out of him by the force of the shots, but he was very much alive. He'd probably have a bruised sternum, but no other damage.

Anger bloomed in his chest.

Connelly and Richardson raced through the doorway and skidded to a stop. Their guns were drawn, both aimed squarely at Bricker.

"How?" Connelly asked.

"He was in the wardrobe." McCandless' voice was even, calm.

Richardson shook his head.

"Unbelievable. The local PD didn't sweep the building?"

"Uh, maybe we could dissect this thing later?" McCandless suggested.

"Sorry."

"It's okay. I'm okay. It's Captain Bricker here who has the problem. He wanted to kill Andy, but that vest did its job. So, now what's he do? Shoot Andy through the head? Solves his problem, but he knows you two will drop him like a load of bricks if he does. Quite a quandary."

"Shut up." He jabbed her in the head with the gun's muzzle. He was sure it was still hot. *Good.*

Pulaski lifted his head and stared at Bricker with wide owl eyes, unblinking and terrified.

"Please don't," he begged.

McCandless acted as if nothing was amiss.

"You should make a decision soon. I'm sure Hank radioed the agents as soon as he heard shots fired. No doubt as soon as they finish up their mozzarella sticks or riblets or whatever, they'll be breaking down the door."

Bravado. Covering up her terror.

"No decision needed. Pulaski's inconsequential, either way. You? You're my ticket out of here. Then, when we're clear of danger, I can waste you. Leave you somewhere to rot, so lover boy can find you and give you a proper burial. If I'm feeling charitable. Or maybe I'll dismember you and make it a challenge."

Connelly charged forward. Richardson stuck out an arm and held him back.

"Leo, no," the older man rumbled.

Bricker laughed.

"Coming through."

He pulled McCandless toward the doorway.

"Connelly, listen to me—stay calm," she pleaded.

"I love you, baby," he answered.

Bricker was preparing to mock the exchange when suddenly his thigh exploded into a hot, wet fireball.

"*Wha—?!*"

His vision swam, and his knees buckled.

Sasha waited for her moment. When Connelly attempted to charge Bricker, she knew she had her opening. Bricker was distracted by Hank and Connelly. She yanked the knife from its holder and drove it like a spear into Bricker's upper thigh, not stopping until she hit bone.

He wobbled on his feet and tightened his grip

on the gun, but he was too late. She'd already wrapped her hands around the barrel.

In a motion she'd once used to disarm her husband, she moved her right hand to the base of the grip and twisted until she heard the bones in Bricker's fingers cracking and splintering.

And just like that, she had control of the gun.

She jammed it into his forehead, right between his eyes.

His bladder gave way and a large wet spot spread across the front of his trousers.

She glanced at Connelly and Hank, who were both still frozen in the doorway.

"Does somebody want to help me out here, or should I just shoot him?"

Hank blinked and sprang into action. He pushed Bricker against the wall and started Mirandizing him.

Connelly gently took the gun out of her hands and pulled her against his chest.

"It's over," he breathed.

41

Sasha snuggled closer to Connelly. Upstairs, the house was quiet. The half-dozen Bennett children were curled up in a half-dozen beds, snoring softly or—in the case of the two littlest—drooling onto their pillows, facedown with their bottoms in the air.

Even Cole had drifted off to sleep, sheer exhaustion overriding the adrenaline that had followed his encounter with his father. She'd popped her head in to check on him earlier. He was sound asleep, with Java burrowed into his armpit as if the cat could tell he needed a companion.

She murmured, a content purr in the back of her throat, and reached across the couch for her wine glass. Connelly shifted his arm and handed it to her.

"Thanks."

He stroked her hair in response.

She took a sip of the Argentinian red and tried not to notice how close its ruby color was to the blood that had squirted from Bricker's thigh.

"You're quiet," she observed.

He moved sideways so he could face her full on and said, "I'm overwhelmed. I'm afraid if I talk, I'll start to cry. I almost lost you."

She shook her head. "Don't say that."

"It's true, Sasha."

"But it's over. He's in custody. We don't have to look over our shoulders any more. Every bump in the night isn't going to make us sit up with our hearts in our throats. He's going back to prison, Connelly. For a very long time. We're safe."

Hank had seen to it that Bricker was transported directly to the Florence Supermax in Colorado. There wasn't a federal prison in the country with a higher level of security.

Connelly's eyes were sad.

"I know. I just ..." he trailed off and pulled her against him, jostling her wine glass.

She rested it on the table and placed her hands on his chest.

"Shhh," she said.

They sat like that for a very long time.

The television played softly—a breathless Maisy informed the late-night news viewers of the day's stunning events, culminating in the daring capture of a dangerous fugitive.

Sasha glanced up to see the footage of Connelly walking her out of Pulaski's office, shielding her from the cameras with his broad shoulders.

Then Hank's face filled the screen, all-business and serious, as he answered Maisy's questions with the artful non-answers that marked him as a federal agent.

Finally, Pulaski came into view, gesticulating wildly as he inflated his role in the day's events to mythical proportions.

"Hey, this is it," Sasha said with a giggle as she grabbed the remote to turn up the volume in time to hear Pulaski proclaim ...

"...is why you can be confident that Big Gun Pulaski will dispatch your ex's support modification request with same fierceness used to dispatch murderous felons." Pulaski looked straight into the camera and nodded firmly.

"So, in other words, he'll pee himself?" Connelly asked.

"That was Bricker," she reminded him.

They laughed together then, a real laugh that came from somewhere deep within and drove away the residual anxiety and worry that were lingering between them.

After a moment, Sasha spoke again. "The kids are going to need permanent guardians."

"Yes."

"I don't know about adoption—that's still down the road a way—but we should put in papers with Judge Kumpar offering to serve in that capacity."

Connelly sat up straighter.

"Do you mean it?" he asked.

"Yes."

"You're sure?"

He searched her face.

She cupped his cheeks with her hands, hoping they were steadier than they felt.

"Take yes for an answer, Connelly."

42

One week later

"All rise. The Honorable Abhinav Kumpar presiding."

Sasha stood between Marsh and Will, waiting for the judge to take his seat and wondering if the butterflies swirling around in her stomach planned to settle down any time soon.

"Good morning."

"Good morning, Your Honor."

"Be seated. Quite an entourage you have, Ms. McCandless," the judge gestured toward the front row of the gallery, where Connelly, Hank, Naya, and all six kids were squeezed in, shoulder to shoulder.

She glanced back at the squeaky clean faces and spotless outfits. She'd been awake since five thirty, brushing hair, ironing shirts, and matching socks.

"Your chambers called and said to bring all the Bennett children, Your Honor."

And Naya and Hank had insisted on coming along.

Connelly spent the better part of his morning jamming booster seats into cars and working out a caravan system that would transport the ten of them to the courthouse. Marsh wisely opted to meet them there.

She figured going forward they should just budget an extra two hours to get anywhere.

"Indeed. So, you're the Bennetts?" the judge smiled at the assembled kids.

"Yes, sir," Cole answered in a booming voice. A chorus of "yeses" followed.

"And this is our Uncle Hank!" Calla added, tugging on Hank's sleeve. She was sitting on his lap, her princess braid tucked over her shoulder.

"Black sheep of the family," Hank cracked.

Judge Kumpar threw back his head and laughed.

"Nice to meet you, Uncle Hank. And you are?" The judge nodded at Naya.

"Naya Andrews, Your Honor. I'm Mr. Volmer and Ms. McCandless' legal assistant and, uh, a friend."

"Naya also just finished her first year of law school," Will offered.

"My condolences," the judge deadpanned.

All the light-hearted jokiness should have put Sasha at ease, but she knew she wouldn't relax until Judge Kumpar officially appointed her and Connelly as the kids' guardians. She wished he'd stop joking around and just get started.

"Okay, let's get to it," the judge said as if he had read her mind.

Marsh straightened his bow tie in anticipation.

"Let me make this easy for you," the judge began. "I see no reason not to accept Ms. McCandless as the trustee of the irrevocable testamentary trust. I understand that Mr. Bricker had planned to object through his court-appointed counsel. However, one consequence of shooting one's court-appointed counsel is that there's not exactly a crowd lined up to take his place. So Mr. Bricker has not formally filed any objection. There's no objection of record, so you're it, Ms. McCandless."

"Thank you, Your Honor. But for clarity, would you consider ruling that even if he were to secure counsel brave enough to represent him, Mr. Bricker lacks standing to contest my appointment in the future?"

A slow smile spread across the judge's face.

"I would indeed, Ms. McCandless. Having read Mr. Volmer's brief on the subject, this Court is convinced that Mr. Bricker has no more standing than any other stranger to the estate. He cannot take under the will because he killed the decedent. And he consented to the termination of his parental rights, so he cannot object on behalf of the minor children."

Sasha snuck a glance behind her to make sure the reference to their father killing their mother hadn't upset the kids. Cole and Brianna were paying rapt attention, but the rest of the kids seemed to be lost in their own thoughts. Or, in the case of Mark, trying to play Minecraft on Naya's smartphone.

"Thank you, Your Honor," Will said.

"So with that out of the way, we can move Ms. Bennett's will into probate just like any other," the judge said, clearly addressing Marsh.

"Very good, Your Honor."

A silence fell over the courtroom.

"Is that it, Your Honor?" Marsh finally asked.

The judge cleared his throat.

"There's one other small matter. Judge Perry-Brown and I went back and forth on which of us should rule on the pending guardianship issue, and we agreed that in the interest of expediency and conservation of judicial resources, I would rule. That said, I've discussed my ruling with her, and she concurs."

This is it. The butterflies in Sasha's stomach picked up speed.

She locked eyes with Connelly, who looked as if he were about to jump out of his skin with anticipation.

Judge Kumpar paused. Then he said, "This Court faced a difficult decision because two highly qualified applications were submitted. In choosing between them, the Court was comforted by the knowledge that all of the applicants care deeply about the Bennett children and will no doubt remain involved in their lives."

Two applications?

Sasha's head was buzzing.

Two?

"Having reviewed the applications, the Court hereby appoints Henry Michael Richardson to serve as the permanent guardian of the six minor Bennett children."

Her brain was still struggling to catch up. *Henry Michael Richardson? Hank?*

Behind her the kids were squealing with excitement and surprise.

She turned around. Connelly sat, unmoving, a stunned expression painted across his face. Her heart seized.

Hank was smiling broadly, but she could see the question in his eyes.

"Thank you, Your Honor. But, I'm sorry, did you say there were two applications?"

The judge looked from Sasha to Connelly to Hank.

Then he said, "The identities of the applicants are confidential, Mr. Richardson."

"Of course."

Connelly shook his head like a dog shaking off water and snapped back to the present. He leaned across the gallery and extended a hand.

"Congratulations, Hank."

Hank shook it. Sasha could see him piecing together the information. Some of the joy dimmed in his eyes.

She hurried to the railing and leaned across it with her arms open, inviting a hug.

Hank hugged her back tightly.

"I'm sorry. I didn't know," he whispered in her ear.

"Don't be stupid," she whispered back. "And don't be sorry."

"Congratulations, guys!" she said to the kids.

"Can you teach Uncle Hank how to make an Elsa braid?" Calla asked.

"Oh, I think Sasha and Leo will be hanging around enough that she can keep that chore for herself," Hank told the girl with a wink to Sasha.

She returned to the counsel table on automatic pilot and started pushing papers into her bag.

"That's all I have," Judge Kumpar said. "Court's dismissed. Ms. McCandless, could I have a word with you and Mr. Connelly in private?"

"Of course, Your Honor," she said.

After the kids tumbled out of their seats, followed by Hank, Naya, Will, and Marsh, the judge gestured for them to approach the bench.

Connelly took her hand in his, and they walked together around the perimeter of the well.

The court reporter snapped her case closed and nodded a goodbye.

When the courtroom was empty, the judge sighed and removed his glasses. He leaned forward.

"I want you to know I think you'll be excellent parents someday. But there are several issues here, not the least of which is your personal history with Mr. Bricker. First and foremost, Ms. McCandless, if you were to serve as both trustee and guardian, that could raise questions of impartiality and self-dealing. It's much cleaner this way."

"Of course, Your Honor," she mumbled.

"We're just surprised that Hank would want to take on a family by himself," Connelly explained to the judge.

Judge Kumpar gave a brisk nod. "Mr. Richardson is both your boss and a friend, isn't that correct?"

"Yes."

"Well, I hope I'm not speaking out of turn here, but you know that he is unmarried and childless, correct?"

Connelly looked offended. "Of course."

"Of course. What you may not know is something Mr. Richardson shared with me when he applied as guardian. He was engaged to a woman, many years ago. About a month before their wedding, she witnessed an armed robbery. This was a wrong place, wrong time situation. She went to the police and gave a statement, offered to testify. At that time, the District of Columbia was basically lawless. It was like the Wild West. The authorities offered her protective custody, but she declined. She had a wedding to plan, after all. Mr. Richardson argued with her to reconsider, but she refused. I'm sure you can tell where this story is going."

"She was killed?" Sasha ventured as her stomach sank to her knees.

The judge nodded sadly. "Gunned down in broad daylight." He cleared his throat. "An autopsy revealed that she was newly pregnant. She probably didn't even know yet, but your friend has lived with that knowledge for a quarter of a century."

Sasha closed her eyes to hold back her tears.

Oh, Hank.

The judge waited a beat and then continued, "So, as you can see, Mr. Richardson has some very personal reasons for wanting to help these particular children who lost their mother in much the same way he lost his fiancée and unborn child. And, if I may offer some unsolicited personal advice, might I suggest you take some time to get your married life settled before you jump into parenthood? I've read enough about your various exploits to know that you have a somewhat ... exciting ... personal life. Wait until things calm down. Get to truly know each other in the fullness of marriage. You're young. You have time."

She stared at the judge. Connelly rubbed his thumb against hers. She nodded, not trusting herself to speak.

43

The next day

"Are you sure you're up for this?" Connelly asked. Worry creased his forehead.

She stopped on the stairs and balanced the cherry pie on her hip.

"Connelly, for the millionth time, I'm *fine.* I think Judge Kumpar had a point. We've only been married for six months. Taking on responsibility for six children would probably have been a bit more than we're ready for."

As if on cue, a shriek rose up from within the house. A blood-curdling shriek, followed by shouting and screaming about whose turn it was to change the channel.

She arched a brow. "See? And Hank's a little bit hard of hearing anyway. He's way better suited for this."

Connelly twisted his mouth into a crooked smile. Then he leaned over and covered her lips with a kiss.

"Maybe. But I think it's time to start thinking about making a baby. If nothing else, I hear it's fun."

He resumed climbing the stairs before she could react.

A baby?

She followed him up on to the porch.

A baby?!

She was still trying to wrap her mind around the thought, when Connelly lifted a finger to ring the bell. The door swung open before he pressed it.

"They're here! They're here!" Leah shouted over her shoulder. Then she launched herself at Sasha, smothering her with a tight hug.

"Careful of the pie," she said, as she hugged the girl back. She wondered how daily doses of affection were going to change Hank. It would be fun to watch.

"Ooh, pie. Is it homemade?" Cole asked, appearing in the doorway.

Connelly tilted his head and waited for her to respond.

"Um ... I'm sure whichever Whole Foods team member made it has a home," she said.

Cole laughed and took the pie from her hands. Before he headed for the kitchen, she reached out a hand to stop him.

"Are we okay? You and I?"

There hadn't been an opportunity since the day in the alley to talk about what had happened.

Cole blushed.

"Yeah. I probably owe you an apology. Hank's set me up with a counselor. We're gonna work through my, uh, father issues."

She hid her smile. *Good for Hank.*

"As long as we're okay. I don't want to have to challenge you to a set of suicides to settle things between us."

He rolled his eyes.

"I should get this to the kitchen," he said.

"You two come with me," Brianna ordered, dragging Sasha and Connelly into the rarely-used formal dining room.

The table had been set—obviously by children,

judging by the random array of silverware. Wild flowers sat in a Mason jar in the middle.

"I picked the flowers," Hal announced.

"They're beautiful," Connelly told him.

Two seats were squished together at the head of the table with light blue balloons tied to their backs.

"You sit there," Leah pointed.

"Isn't Naya the guest of honor? We're celebrating her unbelievable grade point average," Connelly pointed out.

Naya's head appeared in the doorway from the kitchen.

"We have a lot to celebrate," she informed him. "Grades, guardianship, the first salad made entirely of vegetables from Leah's garden. I gotta finish up making this dressing before Carl gets here and starts bragging on my grades again. Now put your butts in the chair." She pointed.

They sat.

"Good call," Mark observed over his shoulder as he queued a playlist on the iPod.

"Dinner music even," Sasha observed.

The kids piled into chairs as the music began. Naya came in from the kitchen, wiping her hands on a dish towel.

"Where's Hank?" Connelly asked.

"And Calla?" Sasha added, scanning the room.

The door from the backyard banged open. Leah clapped her hands. Hal bounced excitedly in his booster seat.

Sasha caught Connelly's eye and made a 'what's going on now?' face.

He shrugged, wide-eyed.

Hank and Calla walked into the room through the kitchen. Hank was a half-step in front of the girl.

"We know you're gonna miss all the fun you have with us," Hal said.

"And Uncle Hank's going to make us go to *school* next year, so we won't be around as much to play," Mark added with a punctuating eye roll.

"So we got you something to remind you of us," Cole said, with a meaningful nod at the baby blue helium balloons bobbing behind their heads.

"Oh my lord, not a baby?" Sasha blurted, her porch conversation with Connelly fresh in her mind.

Peals of laughter rang around the table. Leah and Brianna were laughing so hard they could barely breathe.

"Close," Hank rumbled.

He stepped aside. Calla walked forward holding a leash. Attached to the leash was a fluffy chocolate lab. The dog's paws were way too big for its body. It tripped toward them and nosed Connelly's hand.

"It's a puppy!" Calla squealed, handing the leash to Sasha.

"It *is*," Connelly agreed.

It was definitely a puppy. A very scared, overwhelmed-looking puppy.

"We named him for you," Leah offered.

"They came up with Mocha," Hank explained. "But they agreed that you can change it."

"Mocha's perfect," Connelly announced.

The dog seemed to concur. He launched himself onto Sasha's lap and started nuzzling her ear with his hot, wet nose.

A smile crept across her face. Its twin bloomed on Connelly's lips.

Sasha looked around the room at the joy reflected on each face from the tiniest cherub-cheeked Bennett to Hank's lined and distinguished countenance.

Family, she thought.

She turned back to Connelly and lost herself in his soft gray eyes.

My family.

And then in an instant, his smile vanished, replaced by a horrified expression.

Now what?

"What's wrong?" she asked, suddenly worried.

"Java's going to be livid."

ALSO BY MELISSA F. MILLER

Want to know when I release a new book?

Go to www.melissafmiller.com to sign up for my email newsletter.

Prefer text alerts? Text BOOKS to 636-303-1088 to receive new release alerts and updates.

The Sasha McCandless Legal Thriller Series

Irreparable Harm

Inadvertent Disclosure

Irretrievably Broken

Indispensable Party

Lovers and Madmen (Novella)

Improper Influence

A Marriage of True Minds (Novella)

Irrevocable Trust

Irrefutable Evidence

A Mingled Yarn (Novella)

Informed Consent

International Incident

Imminent Peril

The Humble Salve (Novella)

Intentional Acts

In Absentia

Inevitable Discovery

Full Fathom Five (Novella)

The Aroostine Higgins Novels

Critical Vulnerability

Chilling Effect

Calculated Risk

Called Home

Crossfire Creek

Clingmans Dome

The Bodhi King Novels

Dark Path

Lonely Path

Hidden Path

Twisted Path

Cold Path

The We Sisters Three Romantic Comedic Mysteries

Rosemary's Gravy

Sage of Innocence

Thyme to Live

Lost and Gowned

Wedding Bells & Hoodoo Spells

Wanted Wed or Alive

ABOUT THE AUTHOR

USA Today bestselling author Melissa F. Miller was born in Pittsburgh, Pennsylvania. Although life and love led her to Philadelphia, Baltimore, Washington, D.C., and, ultimately, South Central Pennsylvania, she secretly still considers Pittsburgh home.

In college, she majored in English literature with concentrations in creative writing poetry and medieval literature and was stunned, upon graduation, to learn that there's not exactly a job market for such a degree. After working as an editor for several years, she returned to school to earn a law degree. She was that annoying girl who loved class and always raised her hand. She practiced law for fifteen years, including a stint as a clerk for a federal judge, nearly a decade as an attorney at major international law firms, and several years running a two-person law firm with her lawyer husband.

Now, powered by coffee, she writes legal thrillers and homeschools her three children. When she's not writing, and sometimes when she is, Melissa travels around the country in an RV with her husband, her kids, and her cat.

Connect with me:

www.melissafmiller.com

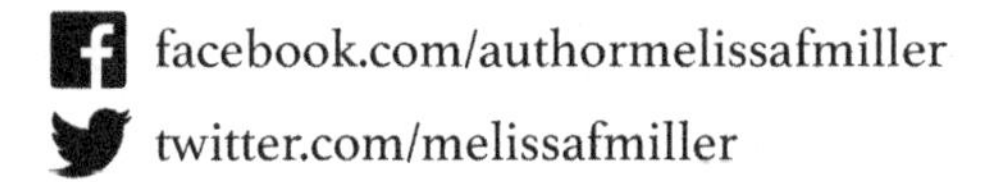

ACKNOWLEDGMENTS

Sincere thanks and appreciation to my editing and proofreading team, especially Curt Akin and Lou Maconi. As always, any mistakes or errors that remain are mine and mine alone. Special thanks to Sasha's Associates for their sustained cheerleading, excitement, and support and to every reader who's ever taken the time to send me a note.

Made in the USA
Coppell, TX
17 January 2024

27811103R00204